"You're right. You're a Kerrigan. I'm a McCloud. But this is business. If I think your horse is trainable, I'll sign the contract."

"Excellent." Rachel's mouth curved in a spontaneous smile of relief and she leaned forward to hold out her hand.

Luke took her hand in his. The combined impact of her smile and the feel of her slim fingers engulfed in his sent a jolt of lust to his groin and a strange longing coursing through his veins. She waited a moment, as if expecting him to say more. When he didn't, she nodded before she turned and walked away.

Luke's gaze followed her, the slight sway of her hips, the faint swing of her dark hair against her shoulders as she crossed the room.

She's going to be trouble.

Dear Reader,

No matter what the weather is like, I always feel like March 1st is the beginning of spring. So let's celebrate that just-around-the-corner thaw with, for starters, another of Christine Rimmer's beloved BRAVO FAMILY TIES books. In *The Bravo Family Way,* a secretive Las Vegas mogul decides he "wants" a beautiful preschool owner who's long left the glittering lights and late nights of Vegas behind. But she hadn't counted on the charms of Fletcher Bravo. No woman could resist him for long….

Victoria Pade's *The Baby Deal,* next up in our FAMILY BUSINESS continuity, features wayward son Jack Hanson finally agreeing to take a meeting with a client—only perhaps he got a little too friendly too fast? She's pregnant, and he's…well, he's not sure what he is, quite frankly. In Judy Duarte's *Call Me Cowboy,* a New York City girl is in desperate need of a detective with a working knowledge of Texas to locate the mother she's never known. Will she find everything she's looking for, courtesy of T. J. "Cowboy" Whittaker? In *She's the One,* Patricia Kay's conclusion to her CALLIE'S CORNER CAFÉ series, a woman who's always put her troublesome younger sister's needs before her own finds herself torn by her attraction to the handsome cop who's about to place said sister under arrest. Lois Faye Dyer's new miniseries, THE McCLOUDS OF MONTANA, which features two feuding families, opens with *Luke's Proposal.* In it, the daughter of one family is forced to work together with the son of the other— with very unexpected results! And in *A Bachelor at the Wedding* by Kate Little, a sophisticated Manhattan tycoon finds himself relying more and more on his Brooklyn-bred assistant (yeah, Brooklyn)— and not just for business.

So enjoy, and come back next month—the undisputed start of spring….

Gail

Please address questions and book requests to:
Silhouette Reader Service
U.S.: 3010 Walden Ave., P.O. Box 1325, Buffalo, NY 14269
Canadian: P.O. Box 609, Fort Erie, Ont. L2A 5X3

LUKE'S PROPOSAL

LOIS FAYE DYER

SPECIAL EDITION®

Published by Silhouette Books

America's Publisher of Contemporary Romance

With much love and thanks to The FairyDusters:
Lisette Belisle, Laurie Campbell, Chris Flynn, Pat Kay,
Allison Leigh, Cheryl Reavis and Myrna Temte.
You guys are the best.

 SILHOUETTE BOOKS

ISBN 0-373-24745-1

LUKE'S PROPOSAL

Visit Silhouette Books at www.eHarlequin.com

Printed in U.S.A.

Books by Lois Faye Dyer

Silhouette Special Edition

* The McClouds of Montana

LOIS FAYE DYER

lives on Washington State's beautiful Puget Sound with her yellow Lab, Maggie Mae, and two eccentric cats. She loves to hear from readers and you can write to her c/o Paperbacks Plus, 1618 Bay Street, Port Orchard, WA 98366.

Dear Reader,

With deep blue sky arching overhead and buttes rising in sagebrush-dotted pastures, eastern Montana is the perfect setting for the McCloud and Kerrigan family feud to play itself out. The McClouds and the Kerrigans have been at odds for over eighty years. Any hope of resolving the family feud was destroyed when teenagers Chase McCloud and Lonnie Kerrigan were involved in an accident that resulted in the death of Chase's good friend Mike Harper. After his father fabricated an alibi for Lonnie, an innocent Chase was sentenced to a juvenile institution for manslaughter and the feud raged anew.

Luke McCloud has always been attracted to Rachel Kerrigan but never allowed himself to pursue the daughter of his family's enemy. When Rachel makes him an offer he can't refuse, in return for his expertise in training her quarter horse, the two are thrown together in a partnership that soon destroys any pretense of indifference. Rachel is equally drawn to Luke and the heat between them quickly blazes out of control. But what will happen when their families learn they've been betrayed?

I've had such marvelous fun exploring the twists and turns of family intrigue, betrayal and pride in this new four-book series. I hope you enjoy Luke and Rachel's story, and that you'll return with me to Wolf Creek, Montana, for the next installment in the McCloud–Kerrigan feud when Zach Kerrigan returns home from a war zone to learn Jessie McCloud has a secret to tell him.

Warmest regards,
Lois Faye Dyer
c/o Paperbacks Plus
1618 Bay Street
Port Orchard, WA 98366
http://www.specialauthors.com

Chapter One

Wolf Creek, Montana
Early Spring, Fifteen Years Earlier

Nothing in Luke McCloud's short fifteen years on earth had prepared him for the shock of abruptly losing his beloved grandfather.

Pain lodged in his chest, right over his heart. His head ached from the gathering pressure of tears behind his eyes, but he refused to let them fall. Instead he stared without blinking at the flower-covered casket. The glossy mahogany box with its gleaming brass handles was suspended over the open grave, waiting to be lowered into the Montana prairie. Beside him, ten-year-old Jessie sobbed, hiccupping as she tried to swallow the sound.

Several feet behind them, a uniformed Montana Department of Corrections officer, hands clasped behind his back, feet spread as he discreetly distanced himself from the proceedings, cleared his throat and coughed.

The wind picked up, sweeping down from the buttes behind the cemetery to ruffle the short spikes of green grass pushing their way up between winter's dried yellow stalks. Lead-gray clouds stretched across the sky from horizon to horizon. Nudged by the wind, they released the rain that had threatened for the past half hour. The shower spattered the small crowd and dampened the black tarp spread over the mound of dirt at one end of the open grave. Moisture pearled on the velvety petals of red roses and lush green leaves resting on top of the casket.

Luke drew in a deep breath, trying to ease the pain in his chest and shift the lump in his throat. The cool air was heavy with the familiar tang of prairie sage blending with the scent of sweet roses and damp earth.

On the far side of the grave, a crowd of black-clad

mourners huddled together, their umbrellas bumping. At the head of the casket, the minister's wife quickly opened a large gray umbrella above her husband's head, stepping close to escape the rain. The somber dome sheltered the gilt-edged pages as the minister read from his leather-bound Bible.

On Luke's left, his little sister Jessie clutched the hand of their older brother, Chase.

Their mother, Margaret, stood on the far side of Chase, her auburn hair a bright flame of color against the deep black of her dress and hat. One hand gripped the arm of Luke's father, John, the other held the handle of a bright red umbrella. The uniformed officer stood several feet behind Chase, a set of handcuffs dangling from the left side of his black gun belt.

Luke ignored the deputy, glancing instead at his mother. Margaret was a strong woman, but losing her father-in-law was devastating, especially coming on the heels of Chase's jail sentence.

The cause of Angus's death was officially listed as pneumonia, but Luke knew his grandfather had died of a broken heart. And for that, he blamed Lonnie and Harlan Kerrigan. Their lies had sent Chase to jail, and Angus had visibly grieved, spending more and more time alone. His death was yet one more reason for Luke to hate the Kerrigans.

The McClouds had feuded with the Kerrigans since 1922, when a crooked poker game cost a McCloud their homestead, 2500 acres of prime land. But this was the first time a McCloud had died because of the enmity between the two families.

Luke's gaze flicked from the casket to the mourners on the far side of the grave, traveling slowly over the familiar faces. His grandfather's widow, Laura Kerrigan-McCloud stood near the front of the group, leaning heavily on a cane as she stared at the casket containing the body of her husband. At her left, his ruddy face set in grim lines, stood Harlan Kerrigan. Luke's glance moved on, registering and dismissing Harlan's sister-in-law, Judith, the wife of his deceased brother, her teenage son, Zach, and young daughter, Rachel standing by her grieving great-aunt's side before searching the crowd beyond.

The one Kerrigan he sought wasn't there.

Lonnie Kerrigan didn't have the guts to show his face at Angus McCloud's funeral, Luke thought, bitterness underscoring a newfound cynicism. His grandfather had married Laura when they were both in their midseventies, and more than once he'd told Luke that the women in the Kerrigan family were beautiful, strong and admirable, but the Kerrigan men couldn't be trusted.

Luke glanced at his grandfather's widow once more, but she was wiping her eyes, the lacy white handkerchief nearly the same color as her pale skin. Luke felt no glimmer of compassion for her grief. He couldn't bring himself to care that the elderly woman had shared his grandfather's life for only four brief years before she was bereaved. Luke had no room in his heart for anything other than his own grief and a deep thirst for revenge.

His gaze moved back to Harlan Kerrigan's niece. Lonnie's cousin Rachel was young, not more than ten or eleven, her thin, childish body wrapped in a black wool coat against the cold April rain. Her bare legs were long and slender. His glance slid impersonally over the girl, marking and filing away in his memory the thick mane of dark hair and black-lashed gold eyes that watched him with solemn compassion.

She has eyes like Lonnie, he thought briefly, as she stared back at him, unblinking. No, not quite, he realized. Lonnie wouldn't have the nerve to face any of us now. It didn't matter how much courage she had. Her last name was Kerrigan, that alone was enough to earn his hatred.

"Our Father, Who art in Heaven..."

Margaret's tear-clogged voice lifted to join the minister's. Luke bowed his head, the girl's golden eyes forgotten as his lips formed the familiar words.

His mother's voice faltered, catching on a sob before it steadied, her fingers tightening their hold on his father's overcoat. Jessie's small, cold hand slipped into Luke's and clung, and he clenched his teeth against the tremors that shook him. He didn't trust his voice not to break so he prayed silently, staring at the ground.

On the far side of the grave, Rachel Kerrigan bowed her head for the Lord's Prayer, but she couldn't resist watching Luke McCloud from behind the shield of her lashes. His features were devoid of expression, his gaze lowered, but she'd caught him looking at Laura moments before. And when that ice blue gaze had left her great-aunt and met hers, she'd been frozen by the fierce anger that leaped to life for a brief moment before he narrowed his eyes and they were once again unreadable.

The crowd around her stirred, shifting and murmuring, and Rachel realized the prayer had ended. She glanced quickly at her great-aunt, but Laura stood motionless, her head bowed in silent prayer. Behind them, two women whispered, their voices growing louder and more distinct.

"Such a shame. Poor John and Margaret."

"They must be heartbroken to lose Angus so soon after that awful business with their son."

Rachel stiffened. Her gaze flew to Laura but she seemed oblivious to the women, lost in her grief.

"Hmph." A third voice joined the first two. "If you ask me, it was Angus that had the broken heart. He was a proud man. It had to be hard on him when his grandson was sent to prison for murder."

Rachel spun to face the three older women. "It wasn't murder," she whispered fiercely. "It was manslaughter. And the car crash was an accident."

"An accident?" The heavyset woman who'd used the M-word pursed her lips and frowned. "That's certainly not what the judge decided. And clearly not what the Harper family believes, since there's not a single one of them here today. Why are you defending young McCloud? He swore your cousin caused the accident. If the judge had believed him, Lonnie would have gone to jail instead of the McCloud boy."

Rachel couldn't tell the gossip that it was possible Lonnie had lied about what happened when Chase McCloud's pickup truck rolled, leaving a third teenager, Mike Harper, dead. In her experience, Lonnie never told the truth if a lie would make his life easier. But her uncle and great-aunt stood within hearing distance and they both doted on Lonnie, stubbornly refusing to admit he was anything less than perfect.

Stymied, Rachel settled for giving the three women a withering glare and turning her back on them.

* * *

Luke echoed his mother and father's murmured amens before he steeled himself as the minister and his wife headed the line of mourners approaching his family. His parents accepted their neighbors' condolences with dignity as they filed past.

He gritted his teeth and met each curious, accusing glance without expression, silently daring them to say anything about his brother. *If they say one word out of line, I swear, I'll hit someone.*

Lonnie Kerrigan's reckless driving had caused the car accident that killed Mike Harper—but Chase was the one in jail. And six months after Lonnie testified under oath that Chase was driving the truck that caused the accident, Angus McCloud suffered a massive heart attack followed by pneumonia. The accident, the teenager's death and the trial resulting in Chase's being sent to a Montana youth correctional facility had devastated the McCloud family.

Luke ignored the passing mourners, his gaze drifting beyond them, locking onto the only five figures that hadn't joined the line shuffling past his parents.

Harlan Kerrigan was shaking off his sister-in-law's hand, clearly growling a refusal at her as he took his aunt Laura's arm and turned his back on the graveside. Zach's unreadable gaze met Luke's before he walked away. The girl hesitated, looking back over her shoulder. Her gaze collided with Luke's, a silent apology in their gold depths, before she turned and hurried after her family.

Harlan helped the widow into the passenger seat and stalked around the heavy green sedan to climb behind the wheel, leaving Zach to open the back door for Judith. The girl scrambled into the back with her mother and brother, barely getting the door closed before the vehicle was moving.

Luke marked the passage of the luxury vehicle as it pulled out onto the graveled county road, following it until it disappeared over the rise of a small hill. Behind him, the officer stepped forward, pulling his attention away from the departing Kerrigans.

"It's time, son." The officer's voice was apologetic but firm as his hand settled on Chase's shoulder.

Resistance roared through Luke, and he tensed, his fingers curling into fists.

Margaret's hand tightened over Chase's forearm, her eyes tortured.

"I have to go, Mom."

"I know." Margaret's voice trembled and caught on a sob. She threw her arms around him and hugged him fiercely. "We'll come see you soon."

"No." Chase returned her tight hug and stepped back. "I don't want you to see me there."

"Chase," she whispered, tears filling her eyes.

"You'll be in prison for two years. Don't ask me to spend two years without seeing you."

Luke couldn't imagine having to endure that long without Chase. His brother was only eighteen months older, and they'd been inseparable all their lives. He held his breath, waiting for him to answer.

"I'm not asking you to never visit, Mom. Just— wait awhile, okay?"

Luke drew a deep breath, struggling for control. Clearly torn by Chase's request, Margaret met his gaze for a long moment before she sighed and gave in. "All right, but don't forget to write."

"I won't."

He bent closer and kissed her soft cheek. Luke saw Chase's eyes close and knew he was dragging in a deep breath, storing away in his memory the smell of her perfume.

Chase held his mother close one last time before he turned to his father and held out his hand. John McCloud pulled him into a tight hug. "Take care, son."

"Yes, sir." He gripped his father, then stepped back and turned to Jessie. "Be good while I'm gone."

"I will," Jessie echoed. Her deep blue eyes were brilliant with the tears that overflowed and slipped down her pale cheeks. She sobbed and flung herself at Chase, wrapping her arms around him, her tight grip desperate.

Chase hugged her, smoothing a hand over the silky crown of auburn hair before he pried her little fists free of his shirt.

Jessie didn't make a sound, but her tears coursed down her face and dripped slowly from the soft, rounded curve of her chin.

Chase's gaze met Luke's, their exchange wordless before they shared a short, hard hug.

Then Chase turned to the officer and held out his wrists. Luke couldn't suppress a growl of protest when the officer snapped the handcuffs in place.

"This is standard procedure, Luke." Chase's look warned him not to interfere. Luke clenched his hands until the short nails bit into his palm as he struggled to contain his rage. The last glimpse Luke had of his brother was a shared glance as the patrol car drove away, leaving the four of them standing by the open grave in the rain.

Fifteen Years Later
Early Spring

The bar was a dive. A man could search high and low through all the cowboy bars in Billings, Montana, and not find a rougher place.

Which was precisely why Luke McCloud had chosen the Bull 'n Bash. He couldn't think of anywhere less likely to be frequented by anyone he knew. Most of his neighbors from Wolf Creek were in Billings for the livestock auctions and he'd rather avoid them, especially Lonnie Kerrigan. He wasn't in the mood for a fight, and a brawl was the usual result when Lonnie was drinking.

Luke sat alone at a round table for four. He'd tilted one of the battered wooden chairs against the rough-cut lumber of the wall at his back and stretched out his legs to prop his boots on the seat of an empty chair. He drank from the longneck bottle of beer in his hand and swept the crowded, dim interior of the tavern with an experienced, assessing eye.

A Dwight Yoakam tune blared from the jukebox near the door, and in the back of the low-ceilinged room, the crack of cue sticks against pool balls was accompanied by grunts of satisfaction or groans of disgust from the players. A haze of cigarette and cigar smoke curled around the cheap hanging lanterns that gave the bar its dim light. Shadows lurked in the corners and partially concealed the doorway leading to a back hall. The Bull 'n Bash was doing a fair amount of business for nine o'clock on a Wednesday night. The bartender was a blonde who'd seen better days, but she smiled and laughed at the jokes from the three old cowboys occupying the worn red vinyl stools at the bar.

The sole waitress was washing glasses. Luke caught her eye and waggled his empty bottle. She smiled and nodded before drying her hands on the white towel tied around her waist.

He watched her grab a full bottle, leave the bar and sashay across the room toward him. She was younger than the bartender, her lush body poured into skintight jeans and an off-the-shoulder white knit blouse. A curly mass of reddish-brown hair brushed her shoulders and tangled in long silver earrings.

"Can I get you anything else?" she asked in a breathy, inviting voice as she set the bottle on the table in front of him.

"No, thanks. How much do I owe you?" She named a figure, not bothering to conceal her interest as he shoved a hand in his jeans pocket, the faded denim pulling tight. He counted out bills and some change, and she cupped her palm to take them. "You're sure I can't get you something else, cowboy?"

"Sorry, honey. Not tonight."

She pouted before smiling. "Maybe some other time."

"Maybe," he acceded with a slow grin.

Placated, she returned to the bar and the stack of dirty glasses.

Luke pulled a silver pocketwatch from his jeans and thumbed open the case, squinting to read the numerals in the dim light. Nine-fifteen. He decided to finish his beer and head back to his solitary bed in the hotel six blocks away. He lifted the bottle to his lips, just as the door to the street opened and a woman stepped inside.

She paused just over the threshold, her thick fall of black hair brushing against her shoulders as she turned her head, searching the room.

There was something familiar about her, but Luke couldn't place her. A slim black dress wrapped her from throat to midcalf, slender ankles and feet tucked into strappy, black leather shoes. A black leather bag the size of a small briefcase was slung over one shoulder. Everything about her said she belonged uptown in the cocktail lounge of Billings's best hotel and not within the rough walls of the Bull 'n Bash. She turned her head, and the dim light from a lantern directly above the door gleamed on her glossy hair.

Luke frowned, his inability to identify her nagging at him.

Look in this direction, he urged silently, wanting to get a clear view of her face.

Then she looked at him, her eyes widening with recognition. He stiffened, slowly lowering the nearly full bottle to the tabletop.

The last time he'd seen Rachel Kerrigan walking down Main Street in Wolf Creek was nearly five years ago, but he'd know those gold eyes anywhere. The usual frustrating mix of lust and slow anger filled him. She faltered in midstride before continuing to weave her way through the tables toward him.

She was only a few steps away before he accepted that it was him she'd been searching the bar to find. She halted on the far side of the table. "Luke McCloud." It was less a question than a statement.

"What are you doing here?"

"I need to talk to you."

Luke let the silence stretch, purposely letting his gaze rake slowly from the top of her dark hair to her feet and back. Her skin was fair, with a sprinkling of tiny freckles across her cheekbones and the bridge of a small, straight nose. She had a soft, full mouth and a square little chin. Conservative pearl-and-gold earrings glinted in her lobes. Slim fingers gripped the leather strap of her purse, the nails neatly manicured.

He'd heard the gossip that the Kerrigans were in financial trouble. It was public knowledge that ninety-year-old Marcus Kerrigan, confined to a nursing home for his final two years of life after suffering a debilitating stroke, had passed away three weeks ago. Rumor had it Marcus had left a will that split his ranch conglomerate equally between his surviving son, his widowed daughter-in-law and his three grandchildren. For generations the property had passed unbroken from father to eldest son and Luke figured the old man's will must have enraged Harlan Kerrigan.

None of which explained why Harlan Kerrigan's niece needed to talk to him, a McCloud. He'd never made a secret of his contempt for the Kerrigans. And despite the unforgettable kiss they'd once shared, he considered her off-limits.

"You need to talk to me," he repeated. "About what?"

"A business proposition. May I sit down?"

She didn't blink under his stare. Luke considered her for a moment, then he lowered his feet to the floor and leaned forward to pull the chair away from the table. She accepted his silent invitation and sat, her back ramrod-straight, ankles crossed, hands folded in her lap, her expression one of resolution.

Luke crossed one ankle over his opposite knee and eyed her, waiting.

Rachel had thought long and hard before approaching Luke McCloud. She knew asking for his help was a long shot, but she was desperate and he was her last hope. Determined though she was, she'd almost turned around and walked out of the tavern when she'd looked across the room and seen him. Stiffening her resolve, she'd forced her feet to carry her across the bar.

But the closer she drew, the more nervous she became.

She'd forgotten how big he was—over six feet tall and heavily muscled, his body honed daily by strenuous ranch work. He sat alone, his long, jeans-clad legs stretched out, ankles crossed, feet resting on the seat of an empty chair. His boots were scuffed and scarred, the black leather showing the unmistakable wear marks of spur straps and metal. His white cotton shirt was fastened up the front with pearl snaps, the long sleeves rolled halfway to his elbows, the tails tucked into the waistband of faded Levi's. His gaze was remote, and she'd seen no flicker of expression cross his face as he'd watched her walk toward him.

His features gave no hint as to what he was thinking, but Rachel doubted his thoughts were friendly ones. She'd planned this conversation with painstaking detail and tried to anticipate every possible reaction from anger, curses or having him walk out of the bar.

No matter what he did, she was determined to follow him and keep talking until he listened. "I have a business proposition," she repeated, "and I hope you'll hear me out before refusing."

He raised an eyebrow, his skepticism obvious, before he nodded.

"I'm sure you've heard my grandfather left a will that was…" She paused, searching for the right word before deciding to opt for frankness. "Let's just say it might be called unusual."

"I heard," he acknowledged. His deep drawl sent shivers of nerves up her spine.

"It's no secret Granddad split the ranch and left specific portions to each of us, nor that the inheritance taxes assessed after his death are staggering. Mother and I can't pay our share of the tax owed and we're on the verge of bankruptcy." He barely reacted to her blunt words; she would have missed the faint narrowing of his eyes if she hadn't been intent on watching him.

"All of you? Or only you and your mother?"

"Only me and my mother. And maybe Zach." Before he could ask why her uncle Harlan and his son Lonnie weren't affected, Rachel continued. "Our only asset capable of paying the tax debt on the land is a three-year-old stud colt out of Misty Morning by Ransom's Regret." The brief flare of interest in his face was quickly erased, but it was enough encouragement for Rachel to continue. "I want to hire you to train him. And to race him." She stopped speaking, holding her breath for his answer, nerves sending her pulse pounding.

"No."

She wasn't surprised. She'd expected a flat refusal, at first. But he hadn't heard the terms. "We don't have cash to pay your fees. But we have the deed to the north section of the ranch."

For a long moment he only looked at her. "You're offering me the deed to the original McCloud homestead instead of cash?"

"Yes."

Chapter Two

"Our families have fought over ownership of the homestead for more than eighty years. Now you're volunteering to sign over 2500 acres of prime land to a McCloud?" Skepticism tinged his deep voice.

"Yes."

He studied her, his gaze fastened on hers as he lifted the bottle and drank, the muscles of his throat moving rhythmically. Rachel refused to look away, despite the instant, vivid memory of that sensual, hard mouth on hers. If she was to have any hope of convincing him to agree to a business relationship, she couldn't let him know he still made her knees weak. She'd never been able to forget the kiss they'd shared when she was seventeen. She'd avoided him ever since. She'd been kissed by other men since. Why hadn't she forgotten the taste and feel of his mouth on hers?

He lowered the bottle. "I can't believe your uncle knows you're doing this."

"He doesn't," Rachel said flatly. "And though he's bound to find out sooner or later, I'd prefer to delay that moment as long as possible."

"If he doesn't know, how can he sign off on the deed?"

"My mother will sign. She has control of the property."

Luke's eyes narrowed over her, his expression sharpening. "Your grandfather left the McCloud homestead to his dead son's widow and not to Harlan?"

"Yes." Rachel refused to elaborate further.

"Your mother moved away from the ranch years ago. I thought she and Marcus were estranged."

His blue stare was unreadable. Rachel had the uneasy feeling he was weighing each word she said. She was an intensely private person, as was her mother, and they'd agreed to keep the difficulties and disagreements they'd had with Marcus, Harlan and Lonnie within the family. How much did she have

to tell Luke to convince him that her mother had the
authority to sign the deed and give him the land?

"My mother wanted my brother and me to grow
up on the ranch, but when Zach was gone and I left
for college, she moved into the house in town she inherited from her parents. She's involved in many
community projects and it's more convenient for her
to live in Wolf Creek rather than twenty miles away
on the ranch."

Rachel knew he wasn't completely satisfied with
her carefully worded explanation. She felt her face
heat as he studied her.

"Why don't you just sell the land to me outright? It
might take a few weeks for me to get the cash, but the
money would be a sure thing. No matter how good
your horse is, racing quarter horses is always a
gamble."

"We considered that," she admitted, pausing to
glance over her shoulder at the bar, buying time to
steady her nerves. The waitress looked distinctly un-
friendly, but Rachel lifted her hand to beckon her
anyway. The woman ignored her, purposely turning
her attention to a cowboy seated on a bar stool, and
Rachel turned back to Luke. She'd anticipated this
question. But, the necessity of telling him a half-
truth went against every principle she held dear. The
whole truth, however, that the will had said her

mother could only accept one dollar from him in return for the property deed, would destroy any hope of his agreeing to train Ransom's Mist. And Luke and Ransom's Mist were the only chance she had to guarantee that the inheritance left to her mother, Zach and herself wasn't lost forever.

"Do you want something to drink?" he asked, glancing past her to the waitress.

"No. I've changed my mind." She drew a deep breath, calmer now, and continued. "Mom and I don't want to give up any more acres than are absolutely necessary. We want to hold the sections that Granddad left us individually and combine them with the land he left to my brother, Zach. He loves ranching and he loves the land."

"Then why isn't he the one talking to me?"

"Because we can't reach him." She thrust her fingers through her hair, tucking the long fall behind her ear. "He's overseas at the moment."

"Hmm." Luke's eyes narrowed. The nervous gesture was the first indication she was anything other than cool and in control. She hadn't once mentioned her cousin Lonnie. Smart woman, he thought. This conversation would have been over if she'd told him Lonnie was the family member she wanted to join forces with. "I had a cousin in the military," he commented, watching her. "In an emergency the family could always reach him through his commanding officer."

Rachel held his stare. "Zach's not military anymore. He left Special Forces to become a munitions consultant with a private company a couple of years ago. Contacting him is difficult at times, if not impossible. His employer wouldn't even tell us what country he's in right now."

"I see." Luke wondered just what kind of black ops mission Rachel's brother was involved in. "How do you think he'll feel about you trading the homestead to a McCloud?"

"He'll understand we have to give up a small part of our inheritance to save the rest."

Luke doubted Zach Kerrigan would understand or agree with the women's decision, but he let Rachel's assertion pass. "It would be a lot easier if you'd just sell me the land outright," he said. "Or sell the whole damn place. My dad would buy it."

"No." Her jaw firmed, her expression stubborn. "Kerrigans have lived on the Bar K since we homesteaded there in the late 1800s. We won't sell. Not unless there's no other possible choice."

Luke could understand her position. McCloud ancestors had settled in the basin the same year the Kerrigans arrived. No McCloud would willingly sell, either.

Which made him question even more why she was willing to trade land for his expertise with horses. Especially this particular piece of land.

"Why do I have the feeling there's more to this than you're telling me," he mused, not really expecting an answer. But the swift lowering of her lashes and the tightening of her grip on the leather straps of her bag told him he was right. What was she hiding? Something about the land—or something about the horse? "Suppose you tell me exactly what the problem is with your horse."

"He's three years old and he's never been ridden."

"And," Luke prompted when she stopped speaking.

"And he won't let anyone close enough to break him."

"That's not unusual. I'm guessing you have reason to believe no trainer can saddle-break him. So cut to the chase and tell me what happened to him."

"When he was a yearling, he was caught in a barbed wire fence." Rachel didn't react to his muttered curse. "By the time my uncle and the hired hand found him, he was down and wrapped in the fence. They had to cut the wire to get him on his feet, and his hide and legs were torn and bleeding in a dozen places. The vet said that given the amount of damage, he'd probably been on the ground and thrashing for some time before he was discovered."

"What the hell was a quarter horse with *his* blood-line doing in an enclosure fenced with barb wire?"

"Harlan was having the metal fences in the horse enclosure painted so he turned Ransom out into the cattle pasture north of the house."

"Huh." Luke's disgust for Harlan's carelessness with a horse as valuable as Ransom must have been written on his face because Rachel stiffened and appeared to steel herself to continue.

"It gets worse."

"Worse?"

"Six months later my uncle hired Troy Armstrong to break Ransom."

Luke swore under his breath.

"Troy had him saddled and bridled when Ransom bucked him off and escaped."

"He knocked down the metal corral fencing? Or he went over the top?"

Rachel shook her head. "No metal fencing. He wasn't in the breaking pen—Troy used the snubbing post in an old wood corral. Ransom went crazy and kicked the half-rotted poles loose, then he crashed through them."

Luke tamped down anger at the trainer's failure to foresee the potentially dangerous situation, and managed to speak without snarling. "How much damage did he do?"

"None to himself but he pretty much wiped out the corral fence. That wasn't a big loss because Harlan rarely uses it, but it was a week before my uncle and Troy could get close enough to rope Ransom and bring him in. He ran loose with the saddle twisted and the reins dangling all that time. When they had him in the breaking pen, it took a long time before they could get him to stand still and allow them close enough to strip the gear off. Ever since, he's been totally unpredictable. He wouldn't let Troy near him. When Troy tried to rope Ransom again to saddle him, Ransom pinned his ears back, bared his teeth and chased him out of the breaking pen."

"Smart horse," Luke commented. "Armstrong is an idiot."

"I wouldn't argue with that assessment," she said with feeling. "Afterward, Harlan turned Ransom loose with the cattle in the open pasture and let him run. He's been there ever since and no one's tried to handle him."

"Why didn't Harlan hire another trainer?"

Rachel glanced around the bar. Luke let the small silence stretch, waiting for her answer but suspecting what it would be.

"I think my uncle decided Ransom wasn't worth the effort."

"But you don't agree?"

"No." Rachel's gaze met his. Conviction rang in her voice. "Ransom's fast. I've seen him run."

Luke didn't know if Rachel's assessment of her horse's speed was accurate. He did, however, know Harlan Kerrigan was bullheaded and stubborn enough to lose his temper and write off a horse who had potential. Maybe the horse really wasn't worth the effort it might take to train and race him, but Luke figured the stud's bloodline alone made it worth a look.

"I have to see the colt before I agree to take him on. And," he added. "I get the land whether your horse wins or not. You'll have to sign a contract."

"Of course." Rachel slipped the bag from her shoulder and unzipped it to pull out a sheaf of papers. "I had our attorney prepare a document."

She held out the stapled legal-size form. He took it, settling back into his chair while he scanned the top sheet, then the second, before looking at her.

"You were pretty confident I'd say yes."

"No." She shook her head. "I hoped you'd say yes. And if you agreed, I knew you wouldn't do it without conditions so I had Mr. Cline put in the ones I anticipated." She gestured at the papers. "I also had him insert a condition I think is important. It's on page three, paragraph two."

Luke turned to page three, and read the second paragraph aloud:

"All parties agree to act in good faith. Luke McCloud shall make all efforts to train Ransom's Mist and enable him to win sufficient races to develop a reputation as a potential stud. Failure to exert such reasonable and expected efforts on the part of Mr. McCloud shall negate the contract in its entirety."

The language was fairly standard, but Luke felt a flash of annoyance that she felt it necessary to have him sign a document affirming he would do his best to train her horse.

"If I don't think I can help your horse after I've looked him over, I won't accept your offer," he said evenly. "If I think he's trainable, and if I think he has a chance of becoming a stud that generates income for you, I'll give him the same time and attention as any other horse I handle."

She flushed, the arch of her cheekbones darkening with color, but her eyes didn't leave his. "You have a reputation for honesty—that's why I approached you instead of someone without our family history. And my sources told me that you're the best trainer in five states. But you're still a McCloud. And

I'm Harlan Kerrigan's niece and Lonnie Kerrigan's cousin. I couldn't ignore the bad blood between our families, nor the possibility that you might feel you have cause to treat our horse differently."

Her words ripped away the veil of pretense between them and sliced with knifelike precision to the heart of the matter. He was John McCloud's son and Chase McCloud's brother. Not only had their ancestors been on opposite sides of a land feud for three generations, but he believed her uncle and cousin had caused his family irreparable harm.

If he agreed to help her, his family would be outraged. Was the long-term gain worth the short-term problems he'd have to face with the rest of the McClouds?

Yes, he decided. He'd deal with his family. Once the deed to the homestead was his and the land legally in McCloud hands, his father, brother, sister and mother would forgive him for agreeing to work with a Kerrigan.

"You're right. You're a Kerrigan. I'm a McCloud. But this is business. If I think your horse is trainable, I'll sign the contract. If not, I won't."

"Excellent." Her mouth curved in a spontaneous smile of relief, and she leaned forward to hold out her hand.

He took her hand in his. The combined impact of

her smile and the feel of her slim fingers sent a jolt of lust to his groin and a strange longing through his veins. Her grip was firm, but her skin was an unexpected combination of roughness and soft silk. Frowning, he turned her hand palm up. Barely healed blisters reddened the skin of her fingers and palm while an angry-looking rope burn marked the center.

She tugged her hand from his and he looked at her, studying the faint streaks of pink on her cheeks.

"You've been working on the ranch?"

"I've been helping Charlie with chores and riding the horses a bit."

Luke wondered just how many hours a day she was working to tear up her hands like that, but decided to let it go.

"I'll be back at my place on Wednesday. Bring your horse by and I'll look him over." He nodded at the legal papers on the table. "I'll have my attorney go over the contract before then."

"Very well." She rose. "Ransom's Mist and I will see you Wednesday."

She waited a moment, as if expecting him to say more. When he didn't, she nodded, the goodbye gesture as brief as his had been, before she turned and walked away.

Luke's gaze followed her slim back, the slight

sway of her hips, the faint swing of her dark hair against her shoulders as she crossed the room. She disappeared from view, and the heavy bar door closed behind her.

She's going to be trouble, he thought. He knew it in his gut.

He'd felt the same when he was twenty-one and Rachel Kerrigan was seventeen, too young and way too innocent for him. Despite his instinctive awareness that she had the potential to screw up his life, he'd been hard-pressed to stay away from her back then.

He'd kissed women before. He'd certainly kissed women since. Why had he never forgotten what her mouth felt like under his?

Luke didn't want to imagine what that said about his feelings for Rachel Kerrigan.

Chapter Three

Rachel walked the short blocks from the bar to her hotel in a daze.

He said yes, she repeated silently as she caught the elevator to her third-floor room, barely aware of the two other people in the lift. The doors opened and she walked down the hall to her room, her fingers trembling in delayed reaction as she swiped her key card and pushed open the door.

She stepped inside and fumbled with the locks before managing to set the dead bolt and slide the security chain into place. The comfortable hotel room had a queen-size bed, and she tossed her purse atop the deep blue spread, kicked off her shoes and dropped onto the edge of the bed.

"He said yes." The whispered words broke the silence in the quiet room. She pushed her heavy mane of hair away from her temples, drawing a deep, calming breath before leaning forward to switch on the bedside lamp and pick up the telephone receiver.

"Hello?" Her mother answered the phone on the first ring, and Rachel knew Judith had probably been pacing the floor for the last hour, carrying the portable phone in her hand and willing it to ring.

"He said yes, Mom."

Judith Kerrigan's swift, indrawn breath was audible. "Thank heavens." Her voice vibrated with relief.

"He has to see Ransom's Mist before he'll sign the contract, but if Luke thinks he has potential, then he'll take him on."

"I wasn't worried about whether Luke McCloud would agree with us that our horse can run," Judith said bluntly. "But I admit I questioned whether he'd consider training a horse owned by a Kerrigan. I'm surprised he listened to you long enough to hear the proposal." Her voice sharpened. "He was polite, wasn't he?"

"Yes, Mom. He was polite."

"Well, that's a relief. He's never been anything

but respectful on the occasions I've seen him in town, but I admit I was worried about you going alone to talk to him."

"We were in a public bar, Mom. I was hardly in any danger."

"Humph. I never thought you were in any physical danger, but your uncle and the McCloud men hold on to that damn feud like dogs with a bone." Judith's tone left no doubt that she disapproved. "It wouldn't have surprised me if Luke had been outright rude to you."

"I half expected him to get up and walk away before I could explain why I wanted to talk to him," Rachel confessed. "Fortunately, he stayed. And he listened." She patted a yawn, overwhelmed with tiredness.

"You sound exhausted, Rachel. I'll hang up so you can get to sleep. When are you coming home?" Judith asked, her tone brisk as she abruptly changed the subject.

"Early tomorrow. I should be in Wolf Creek before lunch."

"Stop at my house before you go out to the ranch. I want to hear all the details of your discussion with Luke."

"I'll do that. Did you hear from Zach today?"

"No, but maybe I will tomorrow. Wherever it is

the company has sent him, surely he'll be in contact with them before too much longer."

"I hope so, Mom." Rachel wasn't as convinced as her mother that Zach would contact them anytime soon. Over the last few years, her brother had often been out of touch for several months at a time, and when he finally wrote or called, he'd wouldn't tell them where he'd been. Whatever Zach did for Connor Security Inc. was top secret. She tried not to think about how dangerous the work might be. "We can't wait for Zach. We have to find a solution that will not only pay our share of the inheritance taxes but also generate future income."

"Unless we want to sell out to your uncle Harlan."

"That's not a possibility for me."

"Nor for me," Judith agreed. "Harlan's always been difficult, but I never anticipated he would act as he has since his father died and we learned the contents of the will."

Judith's heavy sigh conveyed her frustration. "I can't help but wonder why Marcus divided up the ranch but prevented any of us from selling our sections to anyone outside the family, apart from the homestead's 2500 acres. He created an impossible situation when he left us land but no cash."

"I don't think Granddad knew there wasn't any cash." Rachel didn't want to believe her uncle had stripped the cash assets from the ranch during the two years her grandfather was ill. But she couldn't come up with an alternative explanation that made sense.

Judith was silent for a long moment. "You may be right. After your father died and no longer provided a buffer between me and Harlan, I became convinced that he couldn't be trusted. Nevertheless, it's a big leap from family squabbles to an actual crime. But, I can't help wondering how the ranch became so financially unstable in the past couple of years."

"Even if Uncle Harlan juggled the books while Granddad was in the nursing home, I don't know how we'd prove it now. And we still have to find a way to keep our sections financially solvent. Zach's, too, until we can reach him," she added.

"I think we've settled on the best possible alternative," Judith said. "I just wish Zach wouldn't be out of touch for such long periods of time. I worry about him."

"So do I. And I miss him." Her brother's self-imposed exile from Wolf Creek and the Bar K had broken her mother's heart, just as it had Rachel's. Although they kept in touch with phone calls, e-mail and the occasional trip to visit Zach when he was in the U.S., it wasn't enough to keep them from grieving over their separation. She understood why Zach had left and why he'd broken all contact with their grandfather and uncle, but it didn't make her miss him any less. She yawned again. "I'd better get to bed. I want to be on the road early."

"Drive carefully."

"I will. 'Night."

Rachel hung up, switching on the light as she walked into the bathroom. Twenty minutes later, having showered and pulled on lilac cotton pajama shorts with a matching knit top, she climbed into bed, then leaned across the nightstand and turned off the lamp.

She plumped her pillow before lying down, tucking the sheet and light blanket around her waist, before staring upward at the ceiling, where a faint strip of light from the streetlamp outside lightened the dark to gray.

What was it about Luke McCloud that affected her so wildly? One long, slow look from his blue eyes and she was instantly flushed, her nerves strung taut, excitement humming through her veins. She was no longer the naive teenager who'd been fascinated by Luke, despite knowing he was forbidden because he was a McCloud—why did she feel the same overwhelming attraction to him she'd felt at seventeen?

Granted, she thought, she hadn't added a long list of lovers to her sexual résumé since she'd left high school. But she was certainly no longer the innocent virgin who'd been mesmerized by his kiss.

She frowned at the ceiling. No, she wasn't a virgin. But the intimacy she'd shared with her short-term fiancé hadn't held a tenth of the electricity she'd felt earlier when she sat across the table from Luke.

No wonder our engagement drifted into limbo before we called it off, she thought. She and Matt remained friends, and when he'd married a fellow lobbyist six months earlier, Rachel attended the wedding and wished them well without a single twinge of regret. She genuinely liked Matt, but she was relieved that she hadn't been the one standing beside him at the altar, facing a future bound to his.

What did it say about her that one kiss shared with Luke McCloud when she was a teenager had more impact than being engaged to a very nice man she'd dated for three years?

Rachel groaned aloud and determinedly closed her eyes, willing herself to go to sleep.

It did her no good contemplating the reasons why she was so drawn to Luke. The attraction was going nowhere. It couldn't. He was a McCloud; she was a Kerrigan.

Which is roughly equal to Luke and me being on opposite sides of the infamous Hatfield-McCoy feud.

Rachel reached the small community of Wolf Creek just before noon the following morning. The wide, tree-shaded street where her mother lived was quiet, drowsing under the hot sun. She turned into the driveway and parked her little red sports car next to her mother's conservative Lincoln sedan. The long rambler sat amid an expanse of neatly trimmed green lawn edged with flower borders filled with lush hybrid roses and sturdy geraniums, their stems heavy with pink and white blooms. An old oak tree towered over one corner of the lawn, throwing leaf-dappled shade over a large section of thick grass and the sidewalk beyond. Rachel gathered her overnight bag and purse from the car just as her mother stepped out onto the porch.

Judith shaded her eyes with her hand against the hot, bright sunlight.

"Hi, Mom." Rachel closed the car door and started up the brick path that wound across the grass from the driveway to the shallow porch.

"How was the trip?" Judith held open the screen door as Rachel climbed the steps and crossed the porch.

"Fine." She lifted her sunglasses from her nose to perch them atop her head, and stepped past her mother into the entryway. "There was hardly any traffic in Billings when I left this morning, and even the construction work on the highway didn't hold me up very long. I don't think I waited more than ten minutes."

"You were lucky—I sat in line for a half hour the last time I drove south." Judith let the screen door close gently behind her. "I made a pitcher of iced tea this morning and was just about to have lunch. Are you hungry?"

"Tea sounds wonderful, but I ate a sandwich the last time I stopped for gas. I'll pass on lunch." Rachel paused to drop her bag and purse on the low deacon's bench in the foyer and followed her mother down the hall to the kitchen.

Judith waited until they were both seated at the table, sunlight pouring through the window beside them and brightening the comfortable kitchen, before she asked about the meeting with Luke.

"You're sure he wasn't rude to you?"

Rachel shook her head. "Not at all. Not that he was delighted to see me," she added wryly, sipping sweet tea from the frosty glass. "But he didn't refuse to listen, either. He asked some very pointed questions, though, and I hated having to tell him half-truths."

"What did he ask you?"

"He wanted to know why we didn't just sell him the property outright."

"What did you tell him?"

"That selling the homestead wouldn't create ongoing income to keep the ranch afloat."

"And he accepted that?"

"He seemed to." Rachel thought about how they'd parted at the bar in Billings and the way his eyes had narrowed as he'd stared at her during their conversation, as if he knew she was keeping a secret. He can't read my mind, she thought, ignoring the shiver of fear that chilled her. And it's unlikely he'll ever learn the whole truth. "He has no reason to think I was being less than completely honest with him." Saying the words out loud didn't help the uneasiness she felt.

Judith frowned, rubbing the lines drawn by worry between her brows. "I can see why you'd want to conceal the clause in your grandfather's will from Luke. If our finances weren't such a disaster, I'd sign the land over to Luke or Chase, John and Margaret, or even Jessie McCloud tomorrow. Those acres have caused this family nothing but heartache."

Rachel had never confided her misgivings to her mother about the night fifteen years earlier when Mike Harper died on the highway and the Kerrigan-

McCloud feud had blazed out of control. Maybe it was time she did.

"I've often wondered—" She broke off, hesitated, unwilling to upset her mother and unsure how to phrase her concerns, before starting again. "I was shocked when the will was read and we discovered Granddad had split the ranch among the family instead of leaving the property entirely to Harlan. And the clause about the specific section that can only be sold to a McCloud…" She shook her head slowly. "It's very odd and seems completely out of character for Granddad. He loved every acre of this ranch and was adamant about never selling off any part of it. It's occurred to me that in the wording of the will, Granddad came as close as possible—without actually saying the words—to admitting he felt we Kerrigans owed something to the McClouds. Why would he have felt that way unless he knew Lonnie and Harlan had lied about who was responsible for the car accident that killed Mike Harper? Chase McCloud swore that Lonnie was driving that night—what if he was telling the truth and Granddad knew? I can't believe he would have separated the 2500 acres of the homestead from the rest of the property in the way he did unless he believed Chase McCloud was innocent."

"I agree. It's almost as if Marcus is trying to make

reparation from beyond the grave, isn't it?" Judith's voice was weary, her gaze troubled when she met Rachel's. "We can't sell the homestead acres to anyone but a McCloud, and we can't take more than a dollar from them in payment. What does that mean?"

"I think Granddad knew Chase McCloud was innocent and Harlan and Lonnie set him up to keep Lonnie out of jail." Rachel almost whispered the words, her voice hushed.

Judith's eyes squeezed shut, and when she opened them a brief second later, the hazel depths were dark with guilt. "I think you may be right. Which makes it twice as unforgivable that we're using that land as a lure to convince Luke to train Ransom's Mist."

Rachel nodded, her own conscience as tortured as her mother's. "I know. But without Luke to train Ransom, we'll lose everything Granddad left us, and so will Zach. Luke would never help us for any other reason. That land is the only thing we've got that he wants."

"Then we'd better pray he doesn't find out it's already practically his." Judith's voice was grim, exhausted with worry and guilt. "Luke McCloud and his brother are dangerous men. I'd hate to give them any more reason to hate us."

Chapter Four

"He's not gonna take kindly to being loaded in the horse trailer." Charlie Aker's lined face was tanned and weather-beaten beneath his straw cowboy hat. His white eyebrows matched his short-trimmed thick hair, and his pale blue eyes reflected sharp intelligence and wisdom gained over seventy-odd years spent working with cattle and horses.

"I know." Rachel peered through the corral rails at Ransom, the sole resident of the enclosure. "Do you think you and Mom can herd him into the trailer while I stand by to close the gate once he's inside?"

"We can try." Charlie grinned, white teeth

flashing against tanned skin. His eyes twinkled as he winked at her. "You'd better be fast girl, 'cause he's smart."

Her mother's chuckle joined Rachel's laughter as Charlie and Judith swung up on their horses. Rachel opened the gate for them, then walked quickly around the outer perimeter of the corral to reach the loading chute and the horse trailer. At barely 8:00 a.m. the temperature was a comfortable seventy degrees, but the morning sun already promised sweltering heat later in the day. She glanced across the graveled expanse between barn and house and was struck anew with a wave of possessive pride that the ranch, shabby though it was, belonged to her.

Rachel's new home was known as Section Ten of the Kerrigan Conglomerate. The old but comfortable house was part of a cluster of buildings built on a ranch that Marcus Kerrigan had bought and added to his vast holdings. Since Marcus already had an impressive home, which was now Harlan's, the Section Ten buildings had been used over the years to house various employees. Her inheritance from her grandfather consisted of several thousand acres of pasture and rich farmland, the two-story house, a barn, machine shed, corrals and several smaller outbuildings. The pastures were nearly empty, with only a few dozen head of cattle, several older saddle horses, Ransom, and a rangy ten-year-old Appaloosa gelding named Ajax. The horse belonged to Zach, and several years earlier, when he could no longer visit Wolf Creek on a regular basis, he'd given the Appaloosa to Rachel. She'd stabled Ajax at a small ranch outside Helena and ridden him on weekends, trailering him home with her for a few weeks each year when she returned to Wolf Creek to visit her mother. During those vacations, Ajax had been cared for by Charlie, the bowlegged horseman who had worked for her grandfather for as long as Rachel could remember.

The day Rachel told him Marcus had split the ranch and given her Section Ten, Charlie declared he was staying on. She told him she couldn't afford his wages but he said he didn't care. He offered to work for room and board and a promise of future pay when the ranch was in the black. Charlie had taught Rachel and Zach to ride, and they'd both spent many long hours with him as children on their grandfather's huge ranch. Charlie was more like family to Rachel, her mother and brother than their own relatives.

Charlie moved from the ranch house into a small apartment over the tack room in the barn, and Rachel shifted her furniture into the mainhouse. Fortunately, the old bachelor cowboy was neat as a pin and the place was scrupulously clean. Her own feminine, modern furnishings were in stark contrast to the Spartan fifties interior, but Rachel had plans to spruce up the solidly built home when she could afford renovations.

But first we have to get him in the trailer, she thought, forcing her attention back to the corral and Ransom.

Loading the stallion turned out to be far more difficult and time consuming than she'd anticipated. The stallion balked, reared, evaded and generally fought until everyone was equally frustrated.

Rachel wanted to deliver Ransom's Mist to Luke's ranch by 9:00 a.m., but the hands on her watch pointed to ten-thirty when she finally turned off the highway. She drove slowly down the winding gravel road to the house and the cluster of barns, corrals and outbuildings that made up McCloud Enterprises Property #6.

On the seat beside her, carefully tucked into a folder, was the agreement signed by her mother.

Now, if Luke will just sign it, too, she thought. She brushed her hair out of her eyes and sucked in a deep breath as she slowed, parking the borrowed truck and horse trailer in front of the house.

The long, low rambler was neat and tidy, freshly

painted white with black shutters at the windows.
Sprinklers whirled lazily, the arc of water turning the
green grass damp and leaving drops glittering on
the old lilac bush at the far-left corner of the house.
Two tall maples stretched long branches toward the
eaves, their leaves shading the roof from the hot sun.
The oasis of green lawn was fenced with low
wrought-iron posts and rails.

The ranch buildings were located at the end of a
valley and beyond the lush garden stretched pastures
dotted with gray-green sagebrush, rolling upward to
meet the flat-topped buttes that stood in a semicir-
cle behind the house. In the other direction, white-
painted board fences marched in neat, straight lines
away from the horse barn and corrals. Farther out,
fields of oats and rye waved as a breeze rippled the
green stalks.

Rachel switched off the truck engine and slid out
of the cab. The latch on the gate gave easily beneath
her hand, and she passed through, turning to fasten
it behind her. She'd heard about Chase McCloud's
talent as a blacksmith, especially with iron lace
work, and guessed that Luke's brother was the one
responsible for the graceful curves and artistic lines
of the unique gate.

Artistic wasn't a word she would normally have
associated with Chase McCloud, Rachel thought.

She hadn't seen him since his grandfather's funeral fifteen years earlier but the local rumor mill still buzzed with tales of his exploits as a bounty hunter in the years after he was released from jail at age nineteen. The gossip implied he was a dangerous man who'd never forgiven his neighbors for the conviction that had delivered him to Montana's juvenile correction system.

She hoped that didn't mean he would convince Luke not to train Ransom.

She followed the brick sidewalk, climbed two shallow steps and reached the shade of the porch that extended the length of the house.

The screen door was closed but the inner one stood open, allowing her to see down the dim hallway. Somewhere inside the murmur of a radio announcer was followed by the twang of guitars and low growl of Toby Keith and Willie Nelson singing 'Whiskey for my men, beer for my horses.'

The music ceased abruptly the moment she knocked on the door. Boots thudded on wood flooring, and a man walked down the passage to push open the screen door. Rachel took a step back, then retreated two more as he stepped out onto the porch.

Chase McCloud hadn't just grown older. He was bigger, harder and colder than the boy she remembered seeing at his grandfather's graveside. The McClouds were all big men, and she found Luke's height intimidating, but Chase wasn't just tall and broad. He seemed hard as granite, his features remote and bordering on menacing.

Rachel realized he was watching her, waiting for her to speak.

"I'm looking for Luke. Is he here?"

"Down at the barn." He looked past her at the truck and horse trailer parked at the gate before his gaze returned to hers. He didn't say anything further, his expression unreadable.

"Well… I'll drive down there then."

When he didn't respond, she nodded abruptly, spun on her heels, descended the porch steps, marched down the sidewalk, through the gate and climbed into the truck cab. When she glanced back at the house, Chase had disappeared.

Rachel sucked in a deep breath and blew it out. "That man is scary," she muttered as she twisted the ignition key. She shifted into gear and drove past the house and down the gravel lane to park at the barn and corrals.

The big sliding door stood open, and just as Rachel rounded the hood of the truck to search for him, Luke stepped from the barn's dim interior into the bright sunlight. Her stride faltered and she reached out blindly, steadying herself with a hand on the truck's hood.

Like Chase, Luke's sheer size was intimidating, but unlike his brother, he was dangerous to Rachel in so many other ways. Just looking at him made her heart beat faster and heat move through her veins. Her skin seemed more sensitive to the touch of the hot sun and the brush of the faint breeze that lifted the ends of her hair and stroked her body.

There was no question he was the sexiest man she'd ever met. Nevertheless, Rachel was determined to ignore her physical reaction and focus on business.

I need him as a business partner, that's all, she reminded herself. *There won't be anything else between us, regardless of how much my stupid hormones shriek.*

Sunlight highlighted the supple flex of tanned biceps below the short sleeves of his white T-shirt. Faded Levi's rode low on his hips. Torn at the knee, the snug denim faithfully followed the length of powerful, muscled thighs and long legs to end just above the heels of scuffed black cowboy boots.

A straw cowboy hat was tilted over his brow, shading his face. But nothing could conceal the narrow-eyed assessment that rivaled his brother's in intensity.

His ice blue stare snapped her back to reality, and

she realized that she was standing still, gazing at
him like a star-struck teenager. Annoyed, she tucked
her hands into her jeans pockets and stepped
forward.

"Hello, Luke."

"'Mornin'." He nodded his head in greeting, his
gaze lowering in a swift scan from her hair to her
boots and back again.

A lick of fire followed where his gaze touched.
Rachel willed herself not to react when his eyes met
hers and she read the heat there. She resisted the urge
to smooth a hand over the pale yellow T-shirt tucked
into the belted waistband of her worn Levi's.
Repeated washings had faded and shrunk the denim
until the jeans were soft and snug, and Rachel
suddenly wished she'd given more thought to getting
dressed this morning. Maybe she should buy new
jeans that were not quite so close fitting.

On the other hand, she thought, perhaps she
should ignore him. It was downright irritating that
she caught herself wondering fleetingly if he liked
what he saw.

"Ransom's in the trailer." She turned and walked
toward the tailgate. As she passed the back of the
truck, Luke fell in beside her, his long easy strides
carrying him past her. Inside the trailer, the stallion
was enclosed in the front section of the four-horse

carrier, but he wasn't tied and he moved restlessly from one side to the other, clearly stressed. By the time Rachel joined Luke, he'd unlocked and opened the tailgate.

Ransom looked over his shoulder and across the divider at them, his nostrils flaring, eyes widening until a ring of white rimmed the brown. He spun in the narrow space, setting the trailer rattling and swaying, aggression in every flex and bunch of muscles in his powerful body.

"Easy," Luke crooned. "Easy, boy." He eyed the nervous dance of unshod hooves against wood flooring and the small white scars scattered over Ransom's glossy black hide before turning to look at Rachel. "Did he get those scars from the barb wire?"

"Yes."

His jaw tightened, his expression grim as he studied Ransom once more. "He isn't haltered. How much trouble did he give you when you loaded him this morning?"

Rachel thought about lying but decided not to— Luke would find out soon enough just how much Ransom hated to board the trailer. "Some," she admitted, deciding to be as noncommittal as possible.

"Hmm." He considered her for a moment, then closed and latched the gate.

"What are you doing?"

"We'll back the trailer up to the chute into one of the corrals. If he gets antsy coming out, he'll have somewhere to run besides over the top of us." He gestured to the metal rail breaking pen north of the barn and a narrow fenced alley that created a chute leading into it from one side. "Back the trailer over there. I'll open the gates."

Relieved, Rachel nodded and climbed back into the truck. After several minutes of jockeying while Luke guided her with hand signals, she had the trailer lined up with the chute.

"Looks good," he called. Rachel switched off the truck's engine and joined him.

"Before I let him out of there, you'd better tell me exactly what happened to him—the part you left out when I asked you the question in Billings."

Rachel briefly considered telling Luke an edited version of the story. But she knew if he didn't know the facts, he might not be able to help Ransom. So, she opted to be blunt and strictly truthful.

"After Ransom ran loose for a week with the saddle and bridle on him, the men had trouble roping him and bringing him in. They finally got him into the breaking pen, and Armstrong stripped the gear off him before Ransom chased him over the fence. What I didn't tell you was that Charlie, our hired man, was watching and told me Ransom bit a chunk out of Troy's leg as he dove over the top of the fence. If he'd caught him earlier, Charlie thinks Ransom would have tried to do more."

"The horse has better sense than Armstrong." Luke released the tailgate latches. "Is he violent with all humans, or just with Armstrong?"

"I don't know. He's definitely unpredictable."

"Has anyone tried to rope him since he went after Armstrong?"

"Well, no," Rachel admitted. "As I told you, Harlan was so furious that he turned Ransom loose in Section Ten's pasture with the cattle and a few saddle horses and ignored him. Charlie's lived in the house on Section Ten for the last five years so he's been keeping an eye on Ransom, along with the rest of the stock there. He helped Mom and me load him this morning."

"Charlie's still working at Section Ten?" Luke's voice held surprise.

"Yes." Rachel wasn't sure how much Luke knew about the manner in which her grandfather had split the Kerrigan holdings. "Granddad not only left me sole ownership of Ransom, his will also gave me all the land, buildings and stock that make up Section Ten. When I told Charlie, he said he wanted to stay on, and he moved into the apartment when I moved into the main house."

"So Charlie's continued to look after Ransom. How did you get him loaded into the trailer this morning?"

"Charlie, Mom and I ran the saddle horses into the corral last night. Ransom came with them—he always does because Charlie gives them oats when they reach the barn. After they finish eating and he's had a chance to check them for any problems, he separates the horse he plans to use the next day and turns Ransom and the rest loose. Last night we kept Ransom in the breaking pen. This morning Charlie and Mom herded him on horseback into a chute that led to the trailer, and I closed the doors to pen him into the front stall. He didn't exactly cooperate, but we didn't try to rope him so he didn't attempt to bite any of us."

"Why didn't you tell me at the bar in Billings that Ransom attacked Armstrong?"

Rachel met his gaze with a level stare. "If I had, would you have agreed to look him over and consider training him?"

Luke shrugged. "Maybe not."

"I didn't think so. And that's why I didn't tell you." She looked away from Luke into the trailer's interior.

Ransom watched her intently, his ears pricking forward as he shifted from side to side, rocking the vehicle. His liquid brown eyes reflected a sharp intelligence edged with fear and his glossy black hide was flecked with nervous sweat.

"He deserves a chance," Rachel insisted stubbornly.

"Maybe, but he damn sure has two strikes against him already. What makes you think he can run, even if I can keep him from trying to kill his rider?"

"I know he can run." Rachel's voice rang with conviction. "I clocked him two summers ago when I was home for a week visiting Mom. I drove out to the ranch to spend an afternoon with Charlie riding fence. I clocked Ransom playing and racing, and Charlie and I were both stunned at how fast he was. That was before Ransom was caught in the barb wire, but Charlie says he's faster now than he was then."

"It won't matter how fast he is if he refuses to be ridden. A racehorse who won't let a jockey on his back isn't worth a dime."

"I know. That's why I want you to train him."

Luke stared at her for a long moment before he shrugged. "You're a stubborn woman, Rachel Kerrigan. Let's hope this stud is worth it." He gestured to the metal rail fence behind her. "Get outside the pen. I'm going to turn him loose."

Rachel climbed over the rails and dropped down outside, safe from the potential threat of hooves and teeth. Luke released the outside lever that held the gate closed between the front and back sections of the trailer.

For a moment nothing happened. Then Ransom bumped the unlatched gate and it gave way, slamming against the wall and opening an alley to freedom. The trailer rocked violently as a thousand pounds of enraged horse surged forward. He reached the chute, and dirt flew upward as he raced through the narrow opening and into the circle of the breaking pen.

Luke joined Rachel, resting his forearms along the metal rail, ready to jump back if the stallion slammed into the fence. Ransom ran flat-out along the inner rails before veering into the center, screaming defiance at the snubbing post anchored deep in the middle of the dirt oval. He tucked his head between his front legs and bucked, his back legs flying out behind him.

Luke whistled softly. "Well, he can buck. If you can't race him, you can sell him for rodeo rough stock." He glanced down at Rachel. "That's one seriously ticked-off horse you've got there, lady."

"He's scared," Rachel responded, watching Ransom race once again around the inner fence. Each time he approached where they stood, he spun and reversed direction. Dirt flew from beneath his hooves, dust mixed with the foam flecking his sides. She looked at Luke. "Will you work with him?"

"I don't know yet. I told you in Billings I won't take him on if I don't think I can get results."

Rachel bit her lip. She badly wanted to demand that he give her an answer now, but after Ransom's behavior, she was probably lucky he hadn't answered her question with a firm "no." "All right." She turned away from the pen where Ransom was bucking again, stirring up a whirlwind of dust. Pulling open the door to the truck cab, she leaned inside and retrieved the contracts. "Mom's already signed these," she said as she handed him the folder. "I'll call you in a couple of days. Is that long enough?"

He glanced at the package before tossing it, unopened, on a nearby bale of hay. "If there's an outside chance I can train him to behave on a racetrack and win, I should know in a few days. I'll call you."

Luke watched the truck towing the empty trailer as it rattled down the lane, then pulled out onto the highway. The slap of a screen door sounded, and he glanced toward the house just as Chase stepped out onto the porch, his long strides carrying him down the steps and covering the gravel lot between house and barns in moments. Luke turned back to the corral, resting his arms on the fence while he studied Ransom.

Chase leaned his forearms on a rail and watched the stallion in silence, his stance echoing Luke's. At first Ransom raced back and forth, jolting to a halt to spin and run in the opposite direction across the farthest quarter of the pen. When the two men didn't attempt to enter the corral, Ransom slowed, finally stopping to watch them.

"Nice-looking horse," Chase commented.

"Yeah, he's pretty."

"Except for the scars. They look a lot like barbed wire cuts."

"They *are* barbed wire."

Luke didn't turn his head but nevertheless, caught the swift, incredulous look that accompanied his brother's grunt of disgust.

"What owner let that happen?"

"Harlan Kerrigan."

Chase stiffened. "Harlan Kerrigan owns this horse?"

"He owned Ransom when he rolled in barbed wire. He doesn't own him now."

Tension eased out of Chase's frame. "So, who's the current owner?"

Luke looked at his brother and mentally braced himself. "His niece, Rachel."

Chase slowly pushed upright and stepped away from the fence. His eyes narrowed over Luke; his voice dangerously soft when he spoke. "You've got a Kerrigan horse on McCloud land. Why?"

"Because Rachel Kerrigan wants me to train him, and she made me an offer that's damned hard to refuse. She hasn't got cash, so she's going to pay me with the deed to the McCloud homestead."

Chase shook his head in slow disbelief. "I must have heard you wrong. I could swear you said she's giving you the deed to the homestead."

"You heard right. If I agree to train her horse, she'll sign over the land."

"The same land her great-grandfather cheated us out of? The same land McClouds and Kerrigans have been feuding over ever since?"

"Damned hard to believe, isn't it?"

Both men turned to stare at Ransom, the silence lengthening.

"This doesn't make any sense," Chase commented.

"I don't think so, either, but if she's planning to cheat me, I can't figure out how." Luke gestured at the documents Rachel had given him. "She had her lawyer draw up an agreement, and Mrs. Kerrigan signed it. Take a look."

Chase took the folder from atop the bale of hay where Luke had left it and flipped it open. He scanned it, a deepening frown creasing lines between his brows as he read. He reached the last page, then closed the file and dropped it back on the bale. "The contract seems straightforward. But she's a Kerrigan so none of this makes sense. Dad told me Marcus split his holdings between the five surviving Kerrigans instead of leaving it all to Harlan. But that's pretty much all he knew about the situation. What else did the granddaughter tell you?"

"When old Marcus died, he left Rachel this stallion and the Section Ten ranch. She doesn't have the money for the taxes so she plans to race Ransom, and if he wins, retire him to stud. I told her it was a gamble with long odds but she said it's the only chance she has to pay off the inheritance taxes and generate enough income to keep the ranch." Luke glanced sideways at Chase. "There's something odd about the whole situation. Marcus Kerrigan was a rich man. If he cared enough to leave his granddaughter valuable property, why wouldn't he have left her cash so she could stay solvent?"

"Maybe he thought he did."

"What do you mean?"

"Marcus was in a nursing home for the last couple of years, wasn't he? And Harlan ran the company during that time, so he probably had control of the assets. Maybe he siphoned off all the cash and hid it."

"That's the same conclusion I reached." Luke eyed the folder with Rachel's contract. "Which is an interesting theory and would explain why Rachel doesn't have any money. But why did she choose me to train Ransom, and why is she willing to pay me with the homestead deed? Harlan and Lonnie are sure to go ballistic when they find out what she's done." He suddenly remembered Rachel's hope that Harlan wouldn't learn about the trade of land for training expertise. "That reminds me, don't say anything to anyone about my being paid with the homestead acres. She'd like to put off any trouble with her uncle for as long as possible."

"He isn't going to like it. If you decide to do this," Chase said grimly. "You'd better watch your back."

Luke nodded, his gaze returning to Ransom, who stared back, hostility in every line of his compact, muscled body. "In more ways than one," he muttered.

Rachel drove away from the McCloud ranch without the assurance she'd been hoping to find. She'd wanted to return home with good news for her mother. Instead, she still didn't know whether Luke would agree to train Ransom's Mist.

And after watching Ransom go crazy in the breaking pen, she wasn't convinced the stallion would ever let a rider on his back.

Judith was standing on the porch, waiting, when

Rachel drove past, parked the truck and trailer at the barn and walked back to the house.

"How did it go?" She asked as Rachel mounted the steps.

"About as we expected," Rachel admitted. "The bad news is Ransom misbehaved. The good news is he didn't attack Luke or try to bite him." She dropped into a white wicker chair on the porch and heaved a deep sigh. "On the other hand, Luke never let him close enough to try."

Judith rolled her eyes and settled into the matching wicker rocker, her sigh echoing Rachel's. "Did he refuse to train Ransom?"

"No, but he didn't sign the contract, either. He'll call and give us an answer."

"Well, at least he didn't refuse outright," Judith said, her voice optimistic.

"True."

Silence reigned for a long moment while both women gloomily contemplated the lawn and the ranch buildings beyond, drowsing under the hot noonday sun.

"I saw Chase McCloud," Rachel commented at last.

"Did you?" Judith's gaze switched to meet Rachel's, her eyes lighting with interest. "What does he look like?"

"A lot like Luke, only scarier."

"What do you mean, 'scarier'? What did he do?"

"He didn't 'do' anything, in fact, all he really did was direct me to the barn to find Luke. It's more how he looks, and maybe what he didn't say, rather than what he did say."

"Now I'm totally confused," her mother said.

Rachel lifted her hair off her neck, twisted it and knotted it loosely. She knew the silky strands would soon slip and fall free, but for the moment her nape was blessedly cooler with the thick mane pulled higher. "He's a big man, like his father and like Luke, so I suppose his size alone is intimidating. But there's something about him that seems dangerous."

"Well, he *was* in a juvenile center when he was quite young. And I heard he worked as a bounty hunter afterward and was involved in some sort of undercover work."

Rachel lifted a brow. "Do bounty hunters go undercover? I thought cops did that sort of thing…?"

Judith shrugged and lifted her hands expressively. "I have no idea whether bounty hunters do what police do, but the inference was that he was involved in very, very dangerous work."

"Who told you that?" Rachel asked.

"Anna Seeley."

"Oh, Mother," Rachel exclaimed, laughing. "Anna Seeley? Beneath that sweet, little-old-lady face and those snow white curls lurks the biggest gossip and the wildest imagination in the county. I think Anna gets half her stories from the neighbors and the rest she makes up from those true-crime novels she reads."

"Maybe," Judith agreed. "But she swears she heard about Chase McCloud's escapades as a bounty hunter from his mother, Margaret. He spent years engaged in some risky business so I suppose it's no wonder he seems a bit scary."

"Um." A comfortable silence settled. "There's a beautiful wrought-iron fence at the house," Rachel commented idly, mentally comparing the image of the neat McCloud ranch to the shabbier buildings and corrals spread out in front of her.

"Anna told me Chase learned ironwork in the blacksmith shop in prison so maybe he made it."

"Did Margaret tell her that, too?"

"I don't know, Anna didn't say." Judith set the rocker moving slowly back and forth. "She did say that Luke has a reputation for being as tough as his brother."

"She did?" Rachel asked casually. She didn't want her mother to know how curious she was about Luke McCloud's life, but she couldn't resist encouraging Judith to share what she'd heard.

"Of course, I knew that already," Judith went on.

"Chase rarely goes to Wolf Creek but Luke does business there. He belongs to the Stockman's Association and occasionally visits the Cattleman's Bar, and Anna isn't the only person in town who relays scuttlebutt about the McCloud boys. Rumor has it that Luke's been in a few fights at the bar. Most of them happened when he was younger, so it's been several years since he's done anything to stir up the gossips."

"I wonder why neither Luke nor Chase ever married?"

"Hard to say," Judith answered. "I've never heard of either of them going out with anyone in Wolf Creek. Of course, that doesn't mean they don't date elsewhere but it does seem odd that I've never heard rumors. I've seen Luke on occasion, driving through town or walking down the sidewalk, and he's certainly handsome enough. He's well-mannered, too, which is always a plus. The few times I've actually run into him at the bank or Dougan's Pharmacy, he's been polite and that's more than I expected from him, given I was once married to a Kerrigan."

"It's not your fault Harlan is so difficult." Rachel was relieved Luke hadn't been rude to her mother. It boded well for his ability to set aside the feud and agreed to train Ransom. "Did Luke actually speak to you?"

"Oh, yes. We didn't carry on a conversation, but

he held the door open for me, and when I said thank you, he responded by saying 'you're welcome' and tipping his hat."

"I hope we can count on his good manners to continue if he signs the contract."

"I hope so, too. Say what you will about how wild those McCloud boys are, their mother is a stickler for manners and it appears she's had an impact on them." Judith nodded emphatically before glancing at her watch. "Goodness, it's later than I thought." She rose from the rocker and pulled open the screen door. "I have to run home and bake brownies for the bridge club tonight, why don't you come with me?"

"All right." Rachel pushed upright to follow her mother into the house. "I have library books to return. I think I'll pick up some more and maybe drop by the video store and rent a movie or two. The next few days are going to feel like a week while we wait for Luke to call with his answer."

As Rachel predicted, time moved slowly. She extended her normal four hours a day riding and working with Ajax to six or eight before joining Charlie to help with other chores. Still, the minutes and hours seemed to stretch interminably.

Three long days later, Judith arrived early in the morning to help Rachel paint the spare bedroom.

When the phone rang just before noon, Rachel mentally crossed her paint-spattered fingers and picked up the receiver.

"Hello?"

"Is this Rachel?"

The deep voice was instantly recognizable.

"Yes."

"This is Luke McCloud. I've signed the contracts. Do you want me to mail your copy to you?"

A wave of emotion washed over Rachel. "That would be great, thanks," she managed, her voice reflecting none of the sheer relief that turned her legs to water. She looked at Judith and mouthed, "yes." Judith's eyes lit and she clasped her hands together in delight. "When should we meet to discuss details?"

"The contract covers the basics, but if you have questions, I'll be working Ransom tomorrow morning. Come by and we can talk then."

"Very well. I'll do that."

He rang off without saying goodbye, and Rachel thumbed the portable's off switch.

"Well?"

"He said yes," Rachel confirmed, nearly light-headed with the excitement that swirled through her. Judith held her arms out and whirled in a circle.

"Mom," Rachel laughed, startled by her reserved

mother's exuberant reaction. "I've never seen you this excited."

"I don't think I've ever been this excited. I was *so* worried he would refuse." She went still, a small frown growing. "I wonder why he didn't? Did he say *why* he agreed to train Ransom?"

"No. And frankly I'm not sure I should ask him in case it makes him have second thoughts."

"But he's signed the contract so it's too late for him to back out now," Judith reminded her. "And I confess, I'm curious."

"So am I, but I'm so glad he's going to train Ransom I don't care why he said yes, I'm just thankful he didn't say no."

Judith laughed. "I can understand. I wonder how soon he'll have Ransom ready to enter a race?"

"I'll ask him. He said if I have questions I can come by the McCloud ranch tomorrow and we'll discuss them."

"Good." Judith's eyes sparkled. "Let's break out the wine. I stashed a bottle in the fridge this morning so we could celebrate."

"You were that sure he'd agree?"

"No, but I believe in the power of positive thinking."

Rachel followed her into the kitchen, relieved to see her mother so happy. She knew it was a long shot to pin all their hopes on Ransom. He needed to win a race with a million-dollar purse, like the Denver Sweepstakes or the All American Futurity at Ruidoso Downs in New Mexico.

But first he had to be convinced to tolerate a rider.

She crossed her fingers and said a small prayer that Luke McCloud could accomplish a minor miracle.

Rachel was awake past midnight, crunching numbers and calculating what assets she could sell to generate income. From her small trust fund, her 401k and her mother's accounts, she decided there would be just enough to survive until the Denver Sweepstakes. But there might not be enough cash to pay Ransom's entry fee.

Training with Ajax had just become even more important. She'd decided shortly after learning the details of Marcus's will that the big Appaloosa was her one ace in the hole if she ran short of money. Eight years earlier, Zach had ridden Ajax in the local rodeo's Suicide Run—he swore he'd won solely because of Ajax. Anyone could enter the race and the winner's purse was substantial, more than enough to cover the entry fee for the million-dollar Denver Sweepstakes. Despite the years Rachel had spent working in an office in Helena and only being able to ride on weekends, she was determined to work both herself and Ajax until they were ready to challenge the local risk takers in the Suicide Run.

And risk it was. The race was well named—not a year went by without one or more riders finishing with bruises and broken bones.

So she spent hours each day riding and working Ajax, strengthening both of their bodies, building stamina and forging them into a team. Rachel knew the Run was dangerous but she trusted Ajax.

Chapter Five

"I've agreed to train a quarter horse that belongs to Rachel Kerrigan." Luke's gaze swept the members of his family gathered around his parents' massive, oak dining room table. "I thought I'd tell you before you heard it from anyone else."

Varying degrees of shock, surprise and anger moved across the faces of the five other people at the table. "You're doing what?" John McCloud's deep voice reflected the stunned disbelief on his features.

"Now, John…" Margaret admonished. "Remember your blood pressure."

"Well, hell, Margaret." Luke's father shoved away

his nearly empty bowl of low-fat ice cream and fresh strawberries.

"Are you serious?" His sister, Jessie, stared at him over the crown of her son's reddish-brown hair. Perched on the chair between his mother and uncle, little three-year-old Rowdy's head swiveled toward Luke, his dark-blue eyes wide with interest.

"Yes. I am." Luke had purposely chosen the weekly family dinner at his parents' house to make his announcement. He knew there was little likelihood they would agree with his decision, and he'd chosen to face their objections all at once. Chase was silent, his expression grim. "This is business, that's all."

"It's not just business. You're making a deal with the devil when you agree to work with a Kerrigan."

"I don't see it that way, Dad."

"So you're going through with this?"

"If the horse has potential, yes." Luke met his father's gaze without flinching.

The older man's fist hit the table, and Jessie jumped. Rowdy's eyes rounded until he looked like a little owl.

"It's an outrage. Have you forgotten what that son of a—"

"John!" Margaret interrupted. "Not in front of Rowdy."

"Sorry, Jessie," John growled, giving his daughter an apologetic grimace before returning his attention to Luke. "Didn't you learn anything from what the Kerrigans did to this family fifteen years ago?"

"It's Rachel's horse I'll be training, not Harlan's or Lonnie's."

"Huh," John snorted. "What's the difference? They're all Kerrigans."

Chase shoved back his chair and stood. "I need a drink."

"It's only five o'clock," Margaret protested.

John stood, thrusting his fingers through his hair. "I'll join you."

"John…" Margaret's plea was ignored. Her gaze followed the broad backs of her husband and eldest son as they disappeared through the doorway into the living room. She sighed as her troubled gaze moved to Luke. "Lucas, why are you doing this? If there's a good reason for taking on the Kerrigan horse, then tell your father. He can't accept you dealing with those people unless you give him a rational argument."

"This is business, Mom. And who I choose to work with is my decision," he added.

Margaret shook her head, rubbing her fingertips against her temples. "That's all you can tell me?"

"That's all there is."

"Oh, for—" Jessie was clearly frustrated. "Luke, that's not an answer. There's clearly something more. What's the big mystery? All we want is a reason. I'm not as convinced as Dad and Chase that every person in the Kerrigan family is bad, but still…" She stared at Luke, as if she were attempting to see inside his head. "It can't be money. You— or Dad or Chase—could probably buy out the Kerrigans several times over. I heard Rachel quit her job in Helena and came home to take over the ranch her grandfather left her, but there's no livestock with it. Rumor has it she's in deep financial trouble."

Luke didn't answer.

"So is it Rachel? Have you got a thing for her?"

Luke still didn't answer his sister, despite the jolt of guilt her words caused. Jessie probably had no idea how close to the truth her question was. He'd had a "thing" for Rachel Kerrigan since high school, but no one in his family suspected and he had no intention of telling them.

Besides, he told himself, if he lusted after Rachel, it had nothing to do with making a deal for the 2500 acres his family wanted.

A small voice inside his head chuckled derisively.

He ignored it and continued to meet his sister's intent gaze impassively.

Jessie waited several moments until it became obvious that he wasn't going to answer her question.

"You can be *so* stubborn, Luke." She stood, shoving back her heavy oak chair in a frustrated move that echoed her father's and brother's. "Come on, Rowdy. It's time to go home."

She helped him down and took his hand. "I'll call you tomorrow, Mom. I'm sure Luke will help clear the table."

With one last shake of her head at her brother, she left, Rowdy waving over his shoulder at his grandmother and uncle, sitting quietly at the table cluttered with the remains of dinner for six. Melting vanilla ice cream created pools around little islands of red strawberries in the Royal Doulton dessert bowls, and the Waterford crystal water glasses were still half-full.

"You certainly know how to clear a room."

Luke glanced up, startled at the thread of humor lurking beneath his mother's mild tones.

"Sorry, Mom." He gestured at the table with its abandoned dessert bowls and the four empty chairs. "I thought it best to tell everyone at once. Didn't mean to spoil dinner."

"Well, at least you waited until we'd nearly finished." Margaret stood and began to clear the table. She set her great-grandmother's silver salt and pepper shakers next to the matching tea service on the 1880s oak sideboard and circled the big table to collect knives, forks, spoons and glassware. "I would have been really upset if you ran everyone off in the middle of the prime rib."

Luke stood, picked up a stack of dirty bowls and followed his mother into the kitchen. "Does that mean you're not upset?"

Margaret set her handful of silverware and two goblets in the kitchen sink and turned on the faucet. "No." She rinsed silverware, slotted the stainless cutlery into the dishwasher and slid the family silver into soapy water in the second sink, then turned to take the stack of dishes from Luke. "I'm reserving judgment at the moment." She plopped the dishes into the sink. "But you'd better have a good reason for doing this, Luke." She paused, half turning to look him in the eye, her expression determined. "After what Harlan and Lonnie Kerrigan did to Chase, I swore me and mine would never have dealings with anyone in that family again. So you'd better have a monumentally good excuse for even speaking to those people, let alone becoming involved in a business deal."

"Understood." Luke finished helping his mother clean the table and load the dishwasher before saying goodnight and leaving the kitchen.

The wood-paneled living room was empty. The only cowboy present was the Remington bronze

statue of horse and rider resting on the coffee table.
The thick wool rugs scattered across the polished
wood floors muffled the sound of his boots as he
strode across the room and down the hall to his
father's office. But the chair behind the big desk was
vacant, as was the worn leather sofa against the far
wall. Luke's quick search of the barns failed to turn
up either Chase or his father, so he headed for home.

Rachel dreamed about Luke that night.

She was a junior in high school the first time
Luke came to her rescue, three days after her sev-
enteenth birthday.

The fall Harvest Dance was the first big social
event of the school year. She'd known Brian Henley
since sixth grade and when he asked her to be his
date for the dance, Rachel said yes.

That evening, much to her dismay, Brian seemed
to believe that her "yes" meant she was romantically
interested in him. She struggled to wedge space
between them on the dance floor and avoid being
maneuvered into dark corners of the high school
gym. One of his friends had a flask of whiskey and,
despite her protests, Brian laced his punch and hers.
She poured her drink into the potted ficus behind
their crepe-paper-festooned table while he was
talking to friends. When at last they were on their

way home, Rachel was immeasurably relieved because the evening had turned into the longest she'd ever spent.

Just when she was giving thanks that the night was about to end, Brian pulled off the road and parked in a wide, shadowed area halfway between Wolf Creek and the Kerrigan Ranch.

"I have to be home by midnight, Brian," she said, glancing pointedly at her watch. "And it's already eleven-thirty."

"No problem. I'll get you home before curfew." He released his safety belt and, before Rachel could protest, slipped hers free, too.

"Brian, I really need to get home. I think we should go."

"Not yet. Come on, honey," he cajoled. He leaned across the console and grabbed her, wrapping her in a bear hug.

"Stop it, Brian." Rachel turned her face so his kiss missed her mouth and hit her cheek. His breath smelled of sweet punch and whiskey. "I don't want this."

"Don't be that way, Rachel," he coaxed, laughing when she shoved at him.

Brian was a defensive back on the school football team and at seventeen, he already weighed over two hundred pounds, his body solid muscle. When he didn't release her, Rachel pushed harder.

"You've been drinking, Brian, stop it."

"Just one little kiss, and we'll go, I promise."

"No. Let me go."

She twisted and shoved but couldn't budge him. His kisses landed on her temple and cheek until he caught her chin in his hand and held her face still. With one arm free, Rachel pounded her fist against his shoulder, trying to push him away and break his hold as he ground his mouth against hers.

Panic started to filter into her anger when she realized he wasn't going to stop and she wasn't strong enough to make him.

The door at her back suddenly gave way and the dome light came on, its brightness shattering the dark intimacy of the vehicle. A hand closed over Rachel's shoulder.

"What the hell?" Brian lifted his head, squinting at the light.

"Let go of her." The deep male voice was lethal.

Rachel winced as Brian's fingers released her chin and jaw and he returned to his own seat behind the wheel. If the man outside hadn't been holding her steady, Rachel would have fallen backward out of the car.

"Are you all right?"

Breathing in gasps as she dragged in air, she twisted to look over her shoulder. Luke McCloud stood behind her, his hand on her upper arm, his eyes fierce as he searched her face.

"I think so." To her dismay, her voice shook. Her fingers trembled as she lifted a hand to her disheveled hair. The upswept curls had come unpinned in her struggle with Brian and now tumbled around her face.

A muscle flexed in Luke's jaw and his fingers tightened fractionally on her arm. His blue eyes were icier, his demeanor menacing as he looked past her at Brian.

"Get out of the car."

"Hey, I didn't mean anything. I was just…"

Rachel shivered. "Please, I want to go home."

"No problem," Brian moved to switch on the ignition.

"I'll take her home."

Rachel grabbed her evening purse from the floor and slid out of the car, swaying slightly, disoriented by the abrupt movement. Luke caught her waist, steadying her.

"Can you walk?"

"Yes." Her legs no longer felt like rubber, and she took a step back.

His hands fell away from her waist and he nodded abruptly. "My truck's unlocked—I'll be there in a minute."

Rachel nodded, glancing once at Brian's face

before she walked away, her high heels catching in the gravel. Luke's black four-wheel-drive pickup was several yards behind the car, the engine idling with a low rumble. Tugging her narrow skirt up to her thighs, she climbed into the cab and slammed the door. She shivered and rubbed her bare arms, grateful for the blessedly warm air blowing out of the heater vents. Despite the chill, she had no desire to return to Brian's car and collect her light coat.

The truck's headlights were on, illuminating Brian's car and several yards of the surrounding area. Luke stood at the open driver's-side door, Brian in front of him. The sullen, embarrassed expression on Brian's face left no doubt in Rachel's mind that Luke was lecturing him.

The conversation was brief and one-sided. A few short moments later, Luke strode back to the truck and Brian got into his car.

Luke slid behind the wheel and slammed the door. He looked at Rachel and frowned. "Are you cold?"

She realized her arms were crossed, her hands gripping her upper arms. The posture was purely defensive, and she immediately dropped her hands to the small clutch purse lying in her lap. "I was, but the cab is warm. I'm fine," she said when he looked unconvinced.

Brian pulled onto the highway in a bad-tempered

exhibition of speed, his spinning tires spitting gravel before he sped off down the road, leaving them in relative silence except for the low rumble of the truck engine.

Luke didn't look up at the sound and his gaze didn't leave her face. His eyes narrowed. He flicked on the interior light and gently caught her chin in his hand, turning her face toward him.

Rachel winced, her skin tender under his fingers.

His body tensed, though the hand cupping her face remained careful, his thumb smoothing over the spot where Brian had squeezed her jaw. "He hurt you."

"It's a little sore, that's all."

"Any place else?" He scanned her upper shoulders and the brief expanse of throat and collarbones left bare by the gold satin gown.

"No, just my chin and jaw." She tested her lips, faintly puffy and bruised, with the tip of her tongue. "And my mouth is probably bruised, but no cuts."

He cursed softly. "Are you dating him? Or was this a one-time thing?"

"One-time, and the last time," Rachel added fervently. "He's always been a nice guy but some of his friends were drinking tonight and Brian did, too."

"Idiot." Luke's voice held disgust. "You won't be going out with him again, right?"

"No." Rachel gave a shaky laugh. "Definitely not."

"Good."

Silence stretched between them. Luke's eyes turned smoky, and his thumb stroked slowly, compulsively over her skin, almost but not quite touching her lips.

Rachel's heart hammered, her breath shortening.

"I'd better take you home." But he didn't move or take his hand from her face.

"Yes," she said, unable to look away from the sensual curve of his mouth. This was Luke McCloud, self-professed enemy of her family, and the one man she'd dreamed about since he'd stared at her over his grandfather's grave seven years earlier.

His stare locked with hers and he bent his head slowly as if waiting for her to protest. When she remained silent, he brushed his lips against the tender flesh at the corner of her mouth. Rachel caught her breath in an audible sigh. His lashes lowered to screen his eyes as he tilted her chin and brushed soft, careful kisses against the places where Brian's rough grip had hurt her.

Rachel's eyes drifted closed. The gentle, warm touch of his mouth against her chin and jaw healed places inside her she hadn't been aware were bruised.

"Not all men are rough with women." His warm breath touched her lips, his voice husky with emotion. "Forget him."

She lifted weighted eyelids. His face was only inches away, his eyes looking directly into hers. He smelled like clean soap and the faint scent of spicy aftershave, his skin taut over the hard bones of cheek and jaw. Rachel felt a wave of longing so strong it startled her.

Luke pulled back, a curtain dropping over his features. The sensual tide that surged between them immediately ebbed, the spell broken.

"We'd better get you home." He shifted into gear, and the big truck moved forward, gathering speed as they left the gravel parking area for the highway.

Neither spoke until Luke had driven quietly halfway down her lane and stopped, the engine idling.

"I'll let you out here. I'm guessing you don't want your family to know I brought you home."

"That's probably best." Rachel lifted the door handle, gathered her purse and looked at him. His face was shadowed by the dim light from the dashboard gauges. "I don't know how to thank you for tonight, Luke. I don't think I could have stopped Brian."

"You don't have to thank me. Just stay away from him in the future."

"I will." The smile she gave him slowly faded as she realized it was unlikely they'd ever be alone together like this again. "Good night."

"Good night."

Rachel could feel him watching her as she made her way down the dark lane. It wasn't until she reached her parents' porch that she heard his truck reverse back up the long lane to the highway.

Rachel woke from her dream with the sheets and blankets twisted around her. She kicked the coverings to the end of the bed and sat up, glancing at the fluorescent dial of the clock on the bedside stand.

Three in the morning. She groaned and dropped her face into her hands, startled when she encountered dampness.

She'd been crying in her sleep.

So many years had passed since Luke had brushed soft, gentle kisses against her skin and the memory could still make her weep.

Determined to shake off the overwhelming sadness and sense of loss that always accompanied the dream, she slipped out of bed and went downstairs. She needed chocolate, she thought, heading for the kitchen and the brownies her mother baked that afternoon.

Just after ten the following morning, Rachel drove down the lane to McCloud Property #6 and past the house to the barn. She parked her car next to an older, battered pickup truck outside the breaking pen and walked to the metal fence, quietly moving closer until she could rest her forearms on one of the green-painted railings. Luke was inside the corral with Ransom, and the horse was loping around the oval, following the fence. Several yards to her left Luke, his shoulder turned toward the center of the ring, focused all his attention on the stallion. Ransom drew near, and Luke raised his arm in a wide gesture toward the snubbing post at the corral's center. The horse reared, spun toward the fence and raced away in the opposite direction. Luke turned in a small half circle to watch him, and when Ransom drew near from the other side he again raised his arm toward the inside of the corral. Once again, Ransom spun toward the rail to run in the opposite direction. Ears pricked, the horse's attention was trained on Luke but his eyes didn't roll with fear, nor did he seem hostile. Instead, Rachel thought it was as though man and horse were engaged in a choreographed ballet, their movements fluid and graceful, each balancing the other.

She watched silently while Luke worked with Ransom for another ten minutes before turning his back on the stallion and walking toward her.

"Morning, Rachel."

"Good morning." She looked over his shoulder, her eyes widening as Ransom continued to move at a fast lope toward him.

"Ignore him." Luke's voice was quiet.

"But he…" She sucked in a sharp breath when Ransom jolted to a stop barely six feet behind Luke. Then he spun and raced away before turning just as sharply to return, slowing to a walk before halting the same distance away.

Luke didn't look back. Instead he left the corral to pick up a section of an alfalfa bale broken open on the tailgate of the battered old ranch pickup parked beside Rachel's car. He carried the flake of hay back through the gate into the corral, securely latching the metal gate behind him, and walked toward Ransom.

The stallion snorted, spun and raced away. Luke ignored him. He stopped a short distance from Rachel and broke the flake into smaller pieces before filling a canvas holder slung over one of the fence poles. Then he returned to where Rachel stood.

Ransom eyed him with suspicion. Luke glanced at him, then turned to Rachel.

"I can't believe you're in the corral with him," she said, watching Ransom as he shifted and took several steps toward the hay before stopping to eye them. Her heart was only just returning to its regular rhythm but the horse's antics didn't seem to faze Luke. He leaned one shoulder against the metal fence, thumbs hooked casually in the pockets of his faded Levi's. The black T-shirt he wore hugged his torso, straining over the powerful muscles of chest and shoulders. As before, his hooded gaze flicked over her from head to toe, lighting a trail of fire as it passed. Determined to control her reaction, Rachel gestured at Ransom. "He's only been here a little over two days, that's pretty impressive."

"He's tolerating me," Luke agreed, glancing at Ransom once more. The horse didn't run away, but he didn't move closer, either. "But that's about all. We'll see how much progress he's made when I try to put a rope on him."

"That might be the real test," Rachel agreed. "Although you've already succeeded in getting closer to him than anyone else has for months—just being in this corral with him is a major accomplishment."

"He doesn't trust humans," Luke commented, watching as Ransom stepped close enough to the fence post to lip alfalfa from the canvas bag.

The sound of the horse's strong teeth crunching the hay and the sight of green wisps dangling from both sides of his mouth made Rachel smile. "You've won," she whispered to Luke. "He's eating."

"The power of food," Luke said with a half grin, his attention focused on the stallion. Ransom appeared to have forgotten the humans, but each time they spoke, one of his ears would swivel to listen.

"He loves alfalfa, but Charlie says he likes grain even more," she confided. "If you ever need a powerful incentive, try oats with a little molasses."

"I'll keep that in mind," Luke said.

He was interrupted by loud, plaintive braying accompanied by the slam of shod hooves against wood.

Startled, Rachel twisted to look at the barn just in time to see a section of the wall shake before the sweet face and long ears of a molly mule looked out over the closed bottom half of her stall's dutch door. She stretched her neck out and brayed once again.

Ransom lifted his head from the hay and bugled a response.

Rachel's eyes widened. "She's not…?"

"In season?" Luke shook his head. "No. But he seems to like her, so I've been letting her into the corral to share hay with him after I've worked him."

He walked away from Rachel, unlatched the barn door and pulled it open. "Come on out, Daisy."

The little mule picked her way daintily across the corral, giving Rachel a sideways glance from behind long lashes, and joined Ransom at the canvas. The much bigger horse didn't object and within a few short minutes, the hay was gone. Ransom swung his head and looked at Luke. The little mule did the same, her smaller-boned body petite beside the powerfully muscled stallion.

"Don't look now, but I think they want more."

"They're spoiled," Luke said.

Horse and mule seemed to decide that no more hay was forthcoming. Ransom turned and moved away from them to the far side of the corral where blades of grass poked through the space between the rails. He lowered his head and began to graze.

Daisy walked to Luke and nudged his back jeans pocket with her nose.

He pulled out a curry brush and smoothed it over her flank. "You're worse than spoiled, Daisy."

The mule huffed at him, her eyes half closing as he continued to brush her coat.

"How long do you think it will be before Ransom is ready to enter a race?"

"Hard to say." Luke shrugged, glancing at Ransom across the corral. "He's a long way from being ready and even after he reaches the point where he can be ridden, he'll need practice on a small track before we can enter him in the kind of race that has a major purse." He looked at Rachel. "You don't need him to just win a few races. To gain the kind of reputation that will command good stud fees, he needs to win big. That means he has to win at Denver or Ruidoso, and he's a long way from being ready for that."

"Do you think he ever will be?"

"It's too early to say. He's got potential," Luke said. "He's got good conformation, he's fast, he's smart, and he's got the right bloodline. The question is whether he's capable of channeling all the energy and hate inside him into the will to win."

Rachel nodded. She was relieved to hear Luke voice her own assessment of Ransom. "I know he can win."

"You mean you hope he can win," Luke said dryly, his eyes narrowing over her. "Don't be fooled into thinking this will be easy. Even if we can convince him to accept a rider and even if he behaves himself on the track, there are a thousand and one things that can happen to a horse before a big race."

"I know," Rachel said. "I grew up on a ranch."

"Then you know you'd better pray hard for phenomenal luck if we're going to pull this off."

"I will. I do." She corrected herself. She glanced at her watch and pushed away from the rail. "I have an appointment in town. Thanks for answering my questions. Do you mind if I drop by in a few days to see how he's doing?"

"We'll be here," he said.

Rachel realized as she turned onto the highway and sped away toward Wolf Creek that Luke hadn't precisely answered her question. He'd only said he and Ransom would be there. He hadn't confirmed he wouldn't mind if she checked back with him for an update.

She could hardly expect him to welcome the prospect of seeing her. In fact, he probably wished she would stay away and leave him to work Ransom without interference.

But she couldn't just sit at home and wait to hear from him. Too much was riding on Luke's progress with Ransom, and since he hadn't offered to update her every few days, she decided to drive back to McCloud #6 in three days.

Her list of errands was short. Rachel finished loading bags of groceries into the trunk of her car before walking down the sidewalk to Dougan's Pharmacy. Dougan's had the best selection of books and magazines in Wolf Creek and she was in the mood to browse.

She pushed open the heavy glass door and stepped into air-conditioned coolness, sighing with relief as she shifted her sunglasses to the top of her head. An elderly shopper nodded as she walked down the shampoo and cosmetic aisle to the magazine section at the back of the store.

Rachel murmured hello and returned the lady's smile, warmed by the small pleasantry. She'd missed this aspect of living in a small town, she realized.

After college she'd purposely immersed herself in work in Helena, building a life far away from the family difficulties at home. Although she missed Wolf Creek and the life there, she hadn't taken time to wonder why.

Or maybe she'd just refused to think about where her life was going. Now that she was back in the town where she grew up, each passing day made her realize that she'd missed a multitude of things about Wolf Creek. The welcoming friendliness of strangers was only one of the qualities of small-town life that she loved.

She reached the section of shelves holding books and magazines and browsed the rows, picking up and leafing through several women's magazines before returning them to the shelf. Nothing riveted her interest, but she'd nearly decided to buy a fashion magazine when another customer approached.

Rachel glanced up from the magazine's glossy pages, the half smile of polite greeting freezing on her lips when she recognized the woman. Her auburn hair and deep-blue eyes were unmistakable. She was Luke McCloud's sister.

Jessie McCloud was about the same age as Rachel, but they hadn't been in the same school classes, and on the rare occasions when they'd found themselves in the same activity, both had acted as if the other didn't exist.

It appeared Jessie wasn't going to repeat past patterns. She didn't pick up a magazine, nor did she pretend to browse while looking through Rachel as if she didn't exist.

"I understand you've asked Luke to train your horse," she said without preamble.

"That's right," Rachel said, wondering if they were about to become embroiled in an argument that would set the gossips abuzz with speculation.

"It's caused trouble for him with my father."

"I'm sorry." Rachel was sincere. "I wouldn't have asked him if I'd had an alternative, but I needed the best trainer possible, and that's your brother."

Jessie nodded in agreement. "True."

Rachel realized Jessie was nervous. Although her blue gaze met Rachel's with direct assessment and her voice was calm, her left hand gripped the strap of a small leather shoulder purse tightly. Beneath the stylish cream linen business suit, her slim body was tense.

Jessie's fingers tightened further on the brown leather strap. "Rumor has it your brother, Zach, is coming home to run the ranch he inherited from your grandfather."

The last thing Rachel had expected from Jessie was a question about her brother. The McClouds had never made a secret of their dislike of the Kerrigans. "I'm sure Zach will come home as soon as we're able to contact him."

Jessie looked startled. "He doesn't know about your grandfather's death?"

"No, he doesn't, and I'm not sure when we'll be able to tell him."

"Why?"

"He's out of the country at the moment—he's a munitions consultant for foreign governments. The company's CEO can't, or won't, recall him unless it's a life-threatening family emergency. Apparently, his current assignment is top secret."

"I see. Well—" Jessie hesitated before her lips firmed "—I hope there isn't trouble between Luke and your brother when he returns."

"I don't expect there to be any problem, certainly not from Zach."

Jessie hesitated as if to say more. Then she appeared to change her mind, nodded abruptly and walked quickly away, her heels tapping a staccato tattoo against the tile-covered floor.

Rachel's gaze followed her until she pushed open the door and left the pharmacy. *I wonder what that was all about,* she thought. If she didn't know better, she'd think Jessie was worried that Zach might return to Wolf Creek. But that was impossible, of course, Rachel thought, why would Jessie care if Zach were here in Montana or halfway around the world?

Rachel fell into a routine, visiting Luke's ranch every few days for an update and staying awhile to watch him work the stallion. Fortunately, she rarely saw Chase, though she quickly learned that he lived on the ranch with Luke. Ransom made amazing progress, and she was astounded at the difference in his behavior.

Her visits were both pleasure and pain, for each time she talked to Luke, the sexual awareness between them tightened perceptibly. Sometimes she felt as if they were joined by a thread that was being slowly reeled in, drawing them nearer and nearer to confrontation.

Or maybe, Rachel thought, it was only her imagination. Luke watched her but he didn't so much as move an inch toward her while at night she tossed and turned, unable to sleep for the dreams of him.

Zach still hadn't checked in, and both Rachel and her mother were beginning to fret about his safety.

Rachel stayed busy. She worked with Ajax four to six hours a day and rode out with Charlie to care for the small herd of cattle and horses or helped him with various chores. She was taken aback at how rundown her uncle had allowed the once well-cared-for ranch to become. Charlie had a long list of odd jobs that needed to be done, from repairing pasture fences to patching roofs. There was always something to do, and although she hated to see the ranch in this neglected condition, she welcomed the opportunity for physical labor. But even hard work didn't always exhaust her enough to sleep soundly through the night.

Ten days after delivering Ransom to Luke, she spent the morning riding fence with Charlie, looking for downed posts and wire. Fortunately, none required immediate attention and she returned home in time for lunch. Afterward, she showered, changed out of her dusty work jeans into a cool white cotton sundress and drove into Wolf Creek to run errands and pick up a load of miscellaneous items Charlie needed from the feed store. Rachel planned to park the ranch truck at the feed store's loading platform, hand her list to Mr. McGonagle and run her other errands while the truck was being loaded.

Wolf Creek was quiet, its main street drowsing in the early-afternoon heat. Rachel pulled into the alley that ran between McGonagle's Feed and the hardware store next door and drove around to the back. A new pickup truck with the McCloud Ranch logo on the door was already parked at the platform, the bed half-loaded with sacks of grain.

She backed her truck up to the platform, leaving enough room between bumper and dock to lower the tailgate, and switched off the engine. She'd just reached the top step of the stairs that led from ground level to the wooden platform when a man exited the feed store, a heavy bag slung over one shoulder.

He tossed it into the bed of the McCloud truck and turned, wiping the back of his hand across his forehead, stopping in his tracks when he saw Rachel. His eyes widened with surprise before a broad, delighted grin curved his lips.

"Hey, Rach." Mack McGonagle strode toward her, caught her around the waist and swung her off her feet, lowering her to engulf her in a bear hug. "I heard you were back in town. I've been expecting you to come see me—what took you so long?"

"Hi, Mack." Rachel laughed and pushed at his arms. "Let go, you big lug. You're crushing me."

Mack just laughed and squeezed her harder. Then he picked her up again and kissed her cheek with more enthusiasm than finesse before he set her back on her feet and beamed at her.

"Damn, you look good, girl. The city must suit you."

"You don't look so bad yourself, Mack. I hear you're engaged to Cheryl."

"Yup. But you could still change my mind." His

eyes twinkled and he patted his heart theatrically. "You know you'll always be my first love."

Rachel laughed out loud. She and Mack had been best friends since grade school. They'd never been romantically involved, but after Rachel had beat him at arm wrestling, Mack had teased her about being his true love. When neither had a date for their senior prom, they'd attended together and had a great time.

"Think you can load my truck sometime today, Mack, or are you going to be busy for a while?"

Rachel's laughter disappeared. She looked over her shoulder. Luke stood in the open doorway of the feed store, a heavy sack of grain over one shoulder.

His face was cold, remote, but his eyes were blue fire.

"Sure, Luke," Mack said easily. "I was just saying hello to an old friend. You know Rachel, don't you?"

"I know her."

Faded denim jeans covered Luke's long legs, dusty black boots on his feet. A blue cotton work-shirt stretched across broad shoulders, the cuffs folded back. He wore leather gloves, his tense grip pressing finger dents into the heavy feed bag on his shoulder.

Rachel's breathing shortened, and she had to force herself to stop staring at him. *There ought to be a law against any man looking that good.*

Irritated with herself at her heated reaction every time she saw him, she refused to respond to Luke and forced her lips to curve into a smile for Mack as she pulled a sheet of lined note paper from her pocket. "Charlie asked me to have you load some supplies for him, Mack."

"Sure thing, hon." Mack scanned the list. "Don't see any problem—we should have everything he needs in stock."

"Great. I have a few errands to run that might take an hour or less. Do you think you'll be finished by then?"

"Don't see why not."

"Excellent." Rachel patted his cheek. "I won't tell Cheryl you're making passes at strange women."

Mack laughed and winked at her. "Thanks, babe. But just so you know," he called after her as she descended the stairs. "You're breakin' my heart, Rach."

She didn't slow nor turn around, merely laughed and waved a hand in farewell as she rounded the corner of the feed lot and started down the shaded alley.

Luke exited the feed store and stopped dead, halted in his tracks by the sight of Mack McGonagle kissing Rachel Kerrigan. A red haze clouded his vision, and he fought the urge to yank her out of McGonagle's arms.

He managed to keep his voice even, but when Mack said she was an "old friend," Luke couldn't help wonder just exactly what kind of "friends" they were. He didn't believe their connection was platonic. Mack had a reputation for charming the ladies. He'd dated most of the women in Wolf Creek at one time or another, and his engagement to Cheryl Plunkett the month before had surprised everyone in town.

Rachel's glossy dark hair and bare shoulders gleamed under the hot sun, the white sundress faithfully outlining her curves before cinching in at her waist, the short full skirt leaving the long length of her tanned legs bare. Luke couldn't believe any male, including Mack McGonagle, wouldn't walk barefoot over cut glass to have her. Just friends? Not a chance in hell.

It didn't help his temper when she calmly ignored him, smiled at Mack and patted his cheek with easy familiarity.

Luke didn't want to see her kiss him again. He doubted his simmering temper would survive watching her plaster herself against Mack for a second time. He turned his back on them and walked to the edge of the dock to toss the bag of grain into his truck bed.

When he turned around, Mack was disappearing

through the open doors into the feed store's dark interior, Rachel's list of supplies in his hand. Rachel was just rounding the corner into the alley. Two large, dusty handprints marked the back of her white dress.

Luke lost the tenuous hold on his temper. The urge to wipe away the imprint of Mack's hands and replace them with his own was too strong to deny.

It took only seconds for him to reach the alley. Rachel was halfway to the street, nearing the thick trunk of Sally McGonagle's treasured old maple. The big tree was an oasis in the dusty alley, nudging the feed store walls on one side and making drivers veer to curve around the pansy-filled flower bed at its base. Its branches stretched outward, the thick canopy of leaves casting dappled light and shadow over Rachel's slim figure.

"Rachel."

She looked over her shoulder, her eyes widening, and turned to face him. "What?"

"Wait."

Chapter Six

Luke kept walking until only inches separated them. Rachel took a step back, her shoulders nearly bumping the wall of the feed store. She was trapped in the corner created by the wall at her back and the tree on her left, while Luke filled the open space before her. They were hidden from view of any passerby on Main Street by the trunk of the old maple.

Rachel's eyes held a touch of wariness, and Luke knew he was crowding her. He couldn't seem to stop himself. The wall of self-discipline he'd erected to keep space between them had been blown to pieces by the sight of Rachel in another man's arms.

Nevertheless, he didn't want her to fear him, and he struggled to tamp down the surge of fierce relief that she was within touching distance.

"You have dirt on the back of your dress."

"I do?"

Without taking his gaze from hers, he tugged the snug fingers of his right glove loose with his teeth before stripping it off. She caught her breath, watching silently while he repeated the process with his left glove. He tucked them in his back jeans pocket and cupped his hands over her shoulders to gently turn her around. She didn't resist, her body first tensing, then relaxing when he brushed his hand across her back above her waist, dusting away the prints left by Mack.

Luke's fingers slowed, testing the supple warmth of her body as he purposely covered the place where Mack's handprints had been with his own palms before he curved his hands around her waist. Her hair swung forward, exposing her tender neck. The heat of the afternoon intensified the scent of her perfume. Unable to resist, he bent his head and brushed his mouth over the soft skin of her nape.

She gasped, a faint moan that ripped away what little control he had left. He turned her to face him, eased her back against the wall and covered her mouth with his.

There wasn't a gentle preliminary tasting, no

hesitant testing of the fit of lips to lips or body to body. Luke pressed against her soft curves which lifted to adjust to his taller frame. He thrust a hand into her hair to hold her; she wrapped her arms around his neck and opened her mouth under his.

They came together with all the pent-up frustration of weeks of denial. The afternoon heat was mild compared to the furnace that burned between them. Neither were capable of worrying whether they were observed, so it was fortunate they were isolated in the alley.

Mine, Luke thought, his senses intent on the soft, scented skin he touched, the press of her breasts against his chest, the wildly eager response of her lips. He lifted her, nudged her legs apart and wedged his thigh between hers.

She moaned and sucked his tongue into her mouth.

Beyond reasoning, Luke slipped his fingers under the strap of her sundress and tugged it down over her shoulder, baring the upper curve of her breast. He tore his mouth from hers and bent his head, his lips hot against the soft pale skin. Her body trembled beneath his mouth, her pulse pounding as she pressed against him in silent demand.

"…and then Carly said she didn't care if Terry called or not, because…" The feminine voice was interrupted by a peal of laughter.

Rachel stiffened, her hands tightening in his hair. Luke glanced sideways just in time to see two women at the end of the alley where it intersected with the street. He shifted, instinctively blocking their view of Rachel should they turn down the alleyway. But, they passed the entrance and continued down the sidewalk in front of the hardware store, quickly disappearing from sight.

Rachel drew in a deep breath and unlocked her fingers from his hair, lowering her hands to push at his shoulders. He looked down at her but didn't step back.

"What are we doing?" Her voice trembled with shock, her eyes still soft and faintly unfocused, dark with arousal.

Luke eased her dress strap upward, mourning the loss of each visible inch of skin as it disappeared under white cotton. "I've wanted to do this for weeks." He brushed his fingertips over the curve of her cheek, smoothing back a strand of hair to tuck it behind her ear. "Don't tell me you didn't want it, too."

Her chin firmed, her eyes stormy. "I won't."

"So we agree we both want this. The question is, what are we going to do about it?"

"Nothing." She tried to shove him away, and he eased his body weight back, but he didn't release her, nor did she drop her hands from his chest.

"Nothing?" Luke's grip tightened.

"Nothing. We both know this is a mistake and it can't go anywhere."

"Why not?" Luke wondered if she was aware that her body was sending signals contradicting her words. Her small hands rested against his chest just below his shoulders, but she wasn't pushing him away. He pressed against her, chest to thigh, and he felt each faint tremor that swept her, each hurried breath that lifted her breasts and flattened the hard points of her nipples against him. They were still in full view of anyone who happened to walk down the alley from the feed store, but he couldn't make himself release her.

"Because of our families. My mother would be worried sick if she knew about this." She bit her lip, her eyes resolute. "Don't tell me your father or Chase would be any happier, Luke."

"My father and brother don't run my life. I make my own decisions."

"And what about your mother? Your sister?"

Luke frowned. "They don't tell me what to do, either."

"Maybe not, but would you purposely set out to break their hearts?"

"Of course not."

"Then this can't happen again."

"Hell," Luke growled. "Neither one of us planned

for this to happen at all. What makes you think it won't happen again?"

"We're both adults. We can choose what we do."

Luke muttered a curse and narrowed his eyes. "You actually believe what you're saying, don't you?"

"Yes."

He eased his weight from her and stepped back, his hands still resting at her waist while hers dropped from his chest. He instantly missed their soft warmth. "Here's what I think, Rachel. I think this has been brewing between us since we were teenagers, and the most logical thing is to head for the nearest motel and burn it off with a few days in bed." *Maybe a few weeks*, he thought. He doubted a few hours or days would put a dent in the hunger he felt for her. "But I've never forced my attentions on a woman and I don't plan to start with you."

He pulled his gloves from his back pocket. "We'll try things your way. We'll be adult about this. But I don't think this is going away and I'm giving you fair warning—if you act like you're willing, any time, any place, I'm not going to walk away from you again."

He caught her chin in his hand and kissed her hard, feeling the spike of need slam into his gut before he turned and left her.

* * *

Rachel watched him stalk away, back down the alley, until he disappeared around the corner toward the loading dock at the feed store. When she could no longer see him, she slumped against the wall, breathless and thankful for its support since her knees felt as if they were made of rubber.

Pretending to be indifferent to Luke McCloud had been hard enough when she thought the attraction was mostly one-sided. But now that she knew he wanted her, too?

She groaned and dropped her face into her hands.

What had she gotten herself into? This had "disaster" written all over it.

She drew in deep breaths, taking a few moments to compose herself before she smoothed back her hair and pushed away from the wall, checking that her dress was buttoned securely. The tiny compact in her purse reflected pink cheeks and a mouth bare of lipstick, so she slicked color over her lips before tucking the mirror and lipstick back into her purse. Then she squared her shoulders and set off down the alley toward Main Street.

With luck, anyone she met would think the afternoon's ninety-degree heat was the cause of her flushed face.

She loitered over her errands, taking longer than

planned in hopes that Luke would have left McGonagle's before she returned. She heaved a sigh of relief when she reached the feed store to find her truck sitting all alone at the loading dock, the bed piled with Charlie's supplies.

Rachel stopped at the mailbox on the main road before turning down the lane that led to Section Ten's headquarters. Her eyes widened when she leafed through the stack of magazines and letters and found a slim envelope with Zach's writing on it.

She quickly ripped it open and removed two sheets of plain white paper, scanning briefly before her shoulders slumped. The letter didn't mention their grandfather's death or the details of his will.

Zach must have written and mailed this before he read her letter about Granddad. Rachel's hopes fell. Chances were he hadn't received her letter yet.

She turned the envelope over, squinting at the blurred postmark. She could barely make out letters but thought they spelled out Uzbekistan. Rachel shuddered; she didn't want to think about what her brother might be doing in one of the world's most dangerous regions.

She put the truck in gear and drove down the lane, parking the loaded pickup outside the barn next to the empty spot where Charlie usually parked his much-newer truck. The ranch was quiet and empty of life, without even a horse or cow visible in the nearby pasture. Rachel carried her purchases to the house and after checking for phone messages, started her car and drove back to Wolf Creek.

"Mom?" Rachel called as she pulled open the screen door and stepped into her mother's entryway.

"I'm in the kitchen."

Rachel crossed the living room and walked down a short hall to the back of the house. Judith stood at the sink, a trug of fresh flowers on the counter beside her next to a cut-glass vase half filled with yellow and red dahlias.

"What brings you to town?" Her mother continued to clip stems and tuck flowers and greenery in the vase.

"I got a letter from Zach today." Rachel said, dropping her purse on the table. "Unfortunately, he must have written it before our letter with the news about Granddad's funeral reached him."

The relief that had initially lit Judith's face was just as quickly erased by a worried frown. "Oh, no. I was so hoping we'd hear he's on his way home. I get more worried with each day that passes with no news from him."

Rachel slipped an arm around her mother's slim shoulders and hugged her. "I'm sure he's fine, Mom, and I know we'll hear from him soon. Why don't you read Zach's letter while I put the kettle on and make a pot of tea."

Judith patted Rachel's hand where it rested on her shoulder. "Excellent idea. I have some of those little chocolate cookies you like in the tin."

Rachel slipped the letter from her pocket and handed it to Judith. Her mother sat at the table, and Rachel turned back to the stove, retrieved the kettle, then filled it at the sink before switching on the burner and adjusting the flame. While her mother read, Rachel quietly took down cups and saucers and set them on the table, adding a delicate plate piled with cookies from the enameled British tin. She was measuring scoops of loose black tea into the Wedgwood teapot when Judith sighed and folded the pages of the letter, tucking them back into the envelope.

"He didn't say anything that might give us a clue as to where he is."

The kettle whistled shrilly, and Rachel looked sideways at her mother as she switched off the burner and poured the boiling water into the teapot. She returned the kettle to the stove and settled the porcelain lid on the teapot before carrying it to the table. "I think the envelope was postmarked Uzbekistan."

Judith turned the envelope over and studied the stamp and smeared black ink. "It's almost illegible

but I think you're right, I can just make out the
U-z-b-k and *s-t-a-n*."

Rachel studied the downward curve of her
mother's mouth. "I think we should go out tonight
and celebrate."

"Celebrate?" Judith's eyebrows lifted in surprise.
"What are we celebrating?"

"A letter from Zach, I know it doesn't contain the
news we'd hoped for, but nonetheless, it's a letter and
besides, we haven't officially celebrated Luke's
agreement to train Ransom."

"We opened a bottle of wine," Judith said.

"But that's not nearly enough of a celebration.
What do you say we go to The Shadows for dinner?
We'll order chocolate mousse for dessert, drink
some wine, get a little tipsy and drown our worries."

Judith's face broke into a genuine smile. "All
right, let's do it." She glanced at her watch. "We've
just enough time to get changed."

"Excellent." Rachel poured tea into the two
fragile china cups and lifted hers in salute. Her
mother laughed and raised her cup to gently touch
Rachel's.

Rachel and Judith were barely seated at a table
in The Shadows, Wolf Creek's nicest restaurant,
with matching glasses of white wine on the snowy

cloth before them when Harlan appeared in the wide entryway.

Rachel glanced up, saw him scanning the long room and nearly groaned out loud. "Uh-oh. Don't look now, Mom, but Uncle Harlan's here."

Judith glanced over her shoulder and stiffened. "And he's coming our way."

Rachel knew her mother and uncle had long ago agreed to maintain the illusion of a friendly relationship while having as little interaction as possible. Still, the details of her grandfather's will had impacted all of them, and she had no idea whether Harlan would continue to behave himself in public as he had in the past. He had an unpredictable temper hidden beneath his charming and affable facade.

"Hello, ladies."

"Good evening, Harlan." Judith eyed him with a slight smile. "How nice to see you."

"A pleasure as always, Judith. And Rachel." He nodded at Rachel and pulled out a chair, settling his six-foot frame into the comfortable seat with ease.

"Harlan," Rachel murmured in response, apprehension mixing with the hope that his mood would be mellow rather than difficult. Given the circumstances of her grandfather's will, however, she suspected her uncle was rarely in a good mood nowadays.

He dropped his Stetson on the tablecloth and leaned back in his chair, contemplating them. A muscle flexed along his jawline, and the faint smile that curved his mouth didn't reach his eyes. His irises, like Lonnie's, were the Kerrigan-trademark brown with gold flecks. Zach had the same coloring but his eyes were warmer, more gold than brown, and Rachel had always felt Harlan's and Lonnie's were somehow colder.

At the moment, Harlan's gaze was flat, his mouth tight beneath the well-trimmed dark-brown mustache that echoed his thick mane of neatly combed hair. As always, everything about his appearance was rigidly conservative, from the meticulous close shave of his beard to the knife-pleat crease in the gray suit trousers and the glossy sheen of his boots. The pale gray tie had a narrow maroon stripe, coordinating beautifully with white shirt and gray suit jacket.

Still, there was something about him that set off alarm bells in Rachel. A nearly visible aura of anger vibrated the air around him.

Uh-oh. With a flash of insight, Rachel realized why he'd sought them out. *He knows about Luke training Ransom.* She braced herself for the inevitable argument.

"I've heard a rumor that you sold Ransom to Luke McCloud." Harlan's voice was pleasant and his expression one of polite inquiry.

Rachel didn't believe for a moment that her uncle was only mildly interested in her reply. His eyes reflected the rage hidden beneath the thin veneer of casual conversation. "I didn't sell Ransom to Luke," she said carefully. She lifted her water glass and sipped, her eyes never leaving Harlan's.

"Then the horse isn't being stabled at McCloud's place?"

"Yes, he is."

"For what purpose?"

"Luke has agreed to train and race Ransom." Judith put in, her voice calm.

Harlan's face turned red over the slope of his cheekbones. "The hell he will. I refuse to allow it."

"I'm sorry you don't approve of the plan, Uncle, but the decision has been made. The contracts are signed. It's too late to change our minds." Rachel purposely kept her voice even and calm, despite Harlan's visibly increasing anger.

She glanced at her mother and found Judith's expression resolute although her face was paler than her usual healthy color. During her childhood when all of the Kerrigans—Judith, Zach, herself, Harlan and Lonnie all lived under Marcus's roof—Rachel had occasionally seen her uncle fly into a rage and punch holes in the walls or throw things. The outward signs of his rising temper were all too familiar. She noted with misgiving the tightening of his fingers where his hand rested on the white tablecloth, the tensing of his body and the heightened color in his face.

"It's never too late to rethink a bad decision, and contracts can always be canceled." He switched his attention back to Judith. "You're being misled if not purposely lied to and deceived. Why would a McCloud agree to train a horse that belongs to a Kerrigan?"

"Luke McCloud's profession is training quarter horses," Judith replied, without really answering his question. "This is purely a business decision."

Harlan's eyes grew colder. "McCloud business can never be Kerrigan business." He looked at Rachel. "He'll destroy the horse. Is that what you want?"

"I don't think he…" she began.

"You don't think," he interrupted her. "That's always been your problem."

Rachel refused to look away, refused to let him see the sharp stab of pain that sliced into her heart at his cold dismissal. This had always been his strategy, to attack her with words until he made her cry or flee. Her father, Harlan's older brother, had died of cancer when she was only five and as a child, she'd longed for Harlan's approval. But she was no longer that vulnerable child and wouldn't allow him to threaten, manipulate or bully her.

"I hardly think this is the time or the place to discuss this," she said quietly, glancing at her mother. Judith's face was flushed and her eyes looked pained, her hands clasped tightly around the stem of her wineglass, her entire body strung with tension. "In fact, I don't see the need for this conversation at all. Granddad left Ransom to me. What I choose to do with him, and whom I choose to have train him, is entirely my decision."

Harlan pushed back his chair and stood. "No decision that connects a Kerrigan to a McCloud is acceptable. I strongly suggest you reconsider—you won't like the consequences if you don't change your mind. My offer to buy you out still stands, but the longer you put off the inevitable, the lower the price I'm willing to pay."

He picked up his hat, nodded politely at them for the benefit any other diners who might be watching and strode out of the restaurant.

"Well." Judith emptied her wineglass and signaled the waiter for more. "That was unpleasant."

"That's an understatement." Rachel shuddered and followed her mother's example, swallowing the rest of her wine. "I think we were just threatened."

"I *know* we were threatened." Judith's eyes snapped with anger. "Harlan's always been a bully."

"Let's hope making empty threats is all he does,"

Rachel grimaced. "He was bound to discover what we were doing sooner or later but I hoped he'd find out later, much later."

"There isn't anything he can do to stop us," Judith reassured her. "You own Ransom. What you choose to do with him is up to you."

"Right." Rachel drew a deep breath and smiled determinedly. "Let's not let him ruin our evening. We're celebrating."

Judith smiled back just as the waiter arrived with their dinner and refilled their wineglasses. Both women purposely avoided mentioning Harlan's name again.

Two days after Luke kissed her senseless and then walked away from her in the alley, Rachel drove down the lane to his ranch and parked in front of the breaking pen. Luke was inside, sitting on his heels near the snubbing post. Three feet away from him, Ransom and Daisy grazed on a small pile of alfalfa. They looked up when Rachel reached the fence, then calmly went back to eating.

Luke rose and walked toward her, his eyes unreadable as he assessed her from beneath the shade of his hat brim.

"Morning."

"Hello." Rachel was relieved Luke was appar-

An Important Message from the Editors

Dear Reader,

If you'd enjoy reading romance novels with larger print that's easier on your eyes, let us send you TWO FREE HARLEQUIN PRESENTS® NOVELS in our LARGER PRINT EDITION. These books are complete and unabridged, but the type is set about 20% bigger to make it easier to read. Look inside for an actual-size sample.

By the way, you'll also get a surprise gift with your two free books!

Pam Powers

Peel off Seal and Place Inside...

THE RIGHT WOMAN

she'd thought she was fine. It took Daniel's words and Brooke's question to make her realize she was far from a full recovery.

She'd made a start with her sister's help and she intended to go forward now. Sarah felt as if she'd been living in a darkened room and some- one had suddenly opened a door, letting in the fresh air and sunshine. She could feel its warmth slowly seeping into the coldest part of her. The feeling was liberating. She realized it was only a small step and she had a long way to go, but she was ready to face life again with Serena and her family behind her.

All too soon, they were saying goodbye and arah experienced a moment of sadness for all e years she and Serena had missed. But they d each other now, and that's what

She held

Printed in the U.S.A.
Publisher acknowledges the copyright holder of the excerpt from this individual work as follows:
THE RIGHT WOMAN Copyright © 2004 by Linda Warren. All rights reserved.
® and ™ are trademarks owned and used by the trademark owner and/or its licensee.

YOURS FREE!
You'll get a great mystery gift with
your two free larger print books!

GET TWO FREE
LARGER PRINT
BOOKS!

YES! Please send me two
free Harlequin Presents® novels
in the larger print edition, and
my free mystery gift, too. I
understand that I am under no
obligation to purchase
anything, as explained on the
back of this insert.

PLACE
FREE GIFTS
SEAL
HERE

139 HDL EE6G   **339 HDL EFUT**

| |
FIRST NAME   LAST NAME

ADDRESS

APT.#   CITY

STATE/PROV.   ZIP/POSTAL CODE

**Are you a current Harlequin Superromance® subscriber
and want to receive the larger print edition?**
Call 1-800-221-5011 today!

▲ **DETACH AND MAIL CARD TODAY!** ▲

(H-SLPO-03/06) © 2004 Harlequin Enterprises Ltd.

The Harlequin Reader Service™ — Here's How It Works:

Accepting your 2 free Harlequin Presents® larger print books and gift places you under no obligation to buy anything. You may keep the books and gift and return the shipping statement marked "cancel." If you do not cancel, about a month later we'll send you 6 additional Harlequin Presents larger print books and bill you just $4.05 each in the U.S., or $4.72 each in Canada, plus 25¢ shipping & handling per book and applicable taxes if any.* That's the complete price and — compared to cover prices of $4.75 each in the U.S. and $5.50 each in Canada — it's quite a bargain! You may cancel at any time, but if you choose to continue, every month we'll send you 6 more books, which you may either purchase at the discount price or return to us and cancel your subscription.

*Terms and prices subject to change without notice. Sales tax applicable in N.Y. Canadian residents will be charged applicable provincial taxes and GST.

ently going to carry on a normal conversation. Whether he'd remind her of their alleyway encounter was still unknown, but she'd take whatever delay she could get. "How is he today?"

"David rode him for a half hour and he didn't try to buck him off. That's an improvement over yesterday."

"Excellent." Rachel felt a surge of hope. Daisy chose that moment to leave the decimated alfalfa pile and amble close to nudge her muzzle against Luke's shirtfront.

Luke gently pushed her away, rubbed her between her long ears and pulled a chunk of carrot from his pocket. The little mule lipped it daintily from his palm, chewed it noisily and bumped him again.

"Poor thing. She's starving," Rachel said, unable to keep from laughing at the wry look Luke gave her. Daisy's back was noticeably wider than it had been a month earlier.

"Yeah, she's just wasting away," Luke agreed. He took a curry brush from the top of a fence post and began to brush Daisy. The mule leaned into the strokes, her eyes half closing with pleasure.

Rachel hated to destroy the friendly atmosphere, but she had to warn Luke about Harlan's thinly veiled threats. She mentally drew in a deep breath. "My uncle knows you're training Ransom."

Luke stopped brushing the little mule, his eyes narrowing. "And?"

"He's not happy. And he claims you'll do something to harm Ransom."

Luke's look turned wintery. "If that's what you think, why did you hire me?"

"I didn't say *I* believed it," Rachel protested. "I said my uncle believes it. And he threatened me if I didn't cancel our arrangement. Not that I plan to," she added hastily. "But I thought I should warn you, just in case."

"What did he say, exactly?"

"He told me there would be unpleasant consequences if I didn't change my mind about having you train Ransom and then strongly suggested, again, that I accept his counteroffer."

"What counteroffer?"

"Harlan offered to buy us out—both Mom and me. The moment the will was read."

Luke was silent for a moment, his gaze assessing. "So," he said slowly. "Your grandfather didn't leave cash to either you or your mother but he did leave liquid assets to Harlan?"

"No, there was no cash. The entire estate was in land, equipment and livestock."

"Then how can your uncle buy you and your mother's share of the estate?"

"He appears to have personal wealth."

"Hmm." Luke's face reflected his disbelief, but he said nothing more.

Rachel was relieved when he didn't question her further. She suspected her uncle had built up his personal bank accounts by draining her grandfather's estate, but she had no real proof and didn't want to confirm Luke's obvious suspicions. "Have you decided on a track for Ransom's first race?"

"The county fair in Canyon City is in two weeks. I've signed him up." Luke shrugged, muscles flexing beneath the blue cotton covering his shoulders. "No guarantees as to how he'll do, but it's time to test the waters."

"Excellent." Rachel's heart lifted. At last they'd find out if Ransom would run in competition. "Well, I'd better get home, I promised Charlie I'd help him this afternoon."

"Rachel." Luke stopped her as she was turning to leave. "You and I have more than one kind of unfinished business between us. I meant what I said in the alley."

She bit her lip, then turned and walked to her car without comment. As she sped down the gravel lane to the county road, she raised a cloud of dust.

"Hell." Luke yanked his hat brim lower over his brow and glared at the receding cloud. Rachel had appeared in his dreams to torture him both nights since they'd shared that searing kiss in the hot alley.

Luke slammed his palm on the sun heated metal railing before turning to stalk across the pen to the barn. How long before she gave in to the inevitable and went to bed with him? And how was he going to keep his hands off her until she did? For years she'd been living on the opposite side of the state in Helena, and although he hadn't forgotten her, at least she didn't walk through his dreams every night. Since seeing her in Billings, he hadn't spent one night without dreaming of her. Knowing she was back in the county and living at Section Ten of the Kerrigan ranch, only a short drive away, was torture.

Ignoring what he felt for Rachel Kerrigan had always been a difficult task, and he was through fighting what lay between them. He'd meant what he'd told her the other day.

He wondered how long he'd have to wait before she gave in to the inevitable.

Not long, he vowed. He'd waited enough—and so had Rachel.

Chapter Seven

Two weeks later and 125 miles northwest of Wolf Creek, Rachel turned off the highway directly across from the Canyon City Fairgrounds and parked outside the office of the Sundown Motel. The parking lot ran the length of the one-story building and was nearly filled with cars and pickup trucks.

Thank goodness I made a reservation, she thought as she got out of her car.

The sound of carnival music and the muted roar of the busy midway carried easily across the highway, and she was anxious to learn how Ransom was handling the crowds and the noise.

Unfortunately, the motel desk clerk was busily checking in a small group of guests and it was nearly a half hour before Rachel could drop her overnight bag in her room. She locked the door behind her and walked quickly across the highway to the huge open field used for fairground parking.

Cars, trucks, horse trailers and fifth-wheel trailers of all sizes were lined up in rows, creating uneven lanes within easy walking distance of the bleachers and barns. She had to repeatedly dodge pedestrians and riders on horses, ponies and mules as they drifted back and forth among the vehicles, but at least she reached the corrals that held livestock and horses.

Just past a 4-H building filled with prize sheep and cattle, Rachel located the long single-story barn where the horses were being housed. She veered around a group of giggling preteens eating pink cotton candy from paper cones, the sticky spun sugar smeared on their fingers and chins, and reached the graveled forecourt just in time to hear a loud bray.

Uh-oh, that sounds like Daisy.

She walked faster, weaving through the fairgoers crowding the wide entryway of the building before pausing to search the aisles lined with box stalls left and right. At the end of the barn, she saw Luke standing outside the gate of the last stall. She moved quickly down the center isle, dodging the clusters of people until she reached him.

Ransom was inside the wide, comfortable space, shifting restlessly in the bedding straw that covered the floor. Each time he bumped Daisy, the little mule raised her head from the alfalfa-filled manger and gave him an annoyed look.

"Is he okay?" Rachel asked.

"He's a little nervous."

"No tantrums when you unloaded him?"

"No. But then, I had oats in a bag. Daisy was behind him and she smelled the grain. When he didn't move, she literally shoved him out of the trailer and into the stall."

Rachel smiled with relief. "She's amazing. She's not afraid of him at all."

"That's because he likes her. He tolerates her pushing him around and making demands. If he didn't, he wouldn't let her get away with it."

Rachel studied the little molly mule. She was beautifully colored, a line back dun that shaded to buckskin on her belly and face. Her dorsal stripe was black as were her mane and the zebra stripes on her legs. Rachel's family hadn't owned mules, but she thought the sweet-faced female with her pansy-dark eyes and long ears would have made a perfect pet for a little girl.

"She looks so tiny standing next to Ransom," Rachel murmured.

"I don't think she understands she's smaller than him. She has a lot of attitude. Reminds me of some women I know," Luke added dryly.

Startled, Rachel looked at him. He stood with one black boot planted on the bottom board of the stall gate, his forearms resting along one of the thick slats, his attention focused on the horse. A white cotton T-shirt stretched over his broad shoulders, his biceps tanned and strong below the short sleeves. Levi's covered his long legs and hips, the blue denim faded to white at stress points. A straw cowboy hat was tugged low over his brow. A small smile curved his lips, his profile clean cut against the sunlight pouring through the open door just beyond the stall.

I've got to stop noticing how good he looks, Rachel thought, *or I'll never survive the next few months.* She forced her gaze back to Ransom and Daisy and tried to remember what he'd said.

Oh, yes. Daisy. He'd been talking about Daisy and women he knew.

"Her attitude reminds you of someone? Or the fact she's smaller than him?"

"Both."

"Hmm. I don't think I should ask who that might be."

She felt him glance at her but resolutely kept her gaze on Ransom and Daisy.

"I was thinking of my mother and sister. Who did you think I meant?"

She flicked a glance at him to find him looking at her, and the heat in his eyes stole her breath. The sexual tension she'd carefully pretended to ignore was suddenly palpable, pulsing in the air between them.

Luke's gaze was enigmatic—a half smile curved his mouth. She'd decided during the two-hour drive from Wolf Creek that she would keep as much distance as possible between them except when they had to talk about Ransom. She'd just had ample proof that spending even that much time with Luke was going to test her willpower.

"Women in general."

"Ah." He glanced at his watch. "I have to check on a few details at the race office. As Ransom's owner, you're entitled to be there if you want."

"No, thanks. I think I'll stay here with Ransom for a while."

Luke touched the brim of his hat and strode away, soon disappearing in the throng that crowded the aisle and entryway.

Rachel drew a deep breath. *I can do this,* she told herself. *I just need to focus on avoiding him and keeping all contact polite, friendly but impersonal.*

Daisy snorted. Rachel looked at her. The little molly mule gave her a wise, knowing glance, fluttering her long lashes as if she were reading her thoughts and laughing.

"This will work," Rachel muttered aloud.

Daisy brayed, one short, derisive sound, before turning her attention back to the bits of hay littering the straw-covered floor.

"Oh, what do you know," Rachel told her. "Anyway, you're supposed to be on my side, girls against the guys, right?"

The little mule ignored her, continuing to chew hay.

"You're difficult."

Daisy didn't even twitch her long, furry-around-the-edges ears. Her presence seemed to be having a calming effect on Ransom. He stood quietly, shifting to stretch his long neck and reach the wisps of hay and spilled grain scattered across the bed of thick straw.

Rachel watched the two for a few more moments before she left the barn. The carnival atmosphere was infectious, and she detoured to stroll down the midway. The smells of hot dogs, barbecue beef, grilled onions, cotton candy and roasting peanuts drifted on the air, mixed with the sharp tang of smoke rising from the grill of a hamburger vendor.

The odors joined the faint scent of animals from the barns just behind her.

Rachel loved county fairs and, small though it was, this one was no exception. During grade school, she'd entered her 4-H colts and various school projects in the local Daniels County Fair and brought home several blue ribbons. Her mother always entered a knitting project, a category that was fiercely competitive. Like Rachel, Judith treasured the blue ribbons she'd worked so hard to earn over the years.

"Hey, lady, toss a ball? Three tries for a dollar. Only a dollar. Win a stuffed teddy bear…" the vendor's voice cajoled.

Rachel shook her head and walked on, the man's attention instantly switching to a small group of teenagers directly behind her.

She paused to watch a mother and young daughter climb into a car on the Tilt-A-Whirl and her stomach lurched as it began to move. Carnival rides made her nauseous—she'd never enjoyed the spinning, whirling motion.

"Hello, cousin."

Startled, Rachel looked over her shoulder and froze.

"Hello, Lonnie." She turned fully to face him. "What are you doing here?"

"Dad and I came to watch your horse run." His smile was dismissive, derision coloring his words.

Lonnie was an expert at using his handsome face and a practiced, friendly interest to deceive and manipulate, but he wasn't bothering to use his charm at the moment. With fingertips tucked into his front jean pockets and Stetson pushed back off his brow, his whole demeanor was belligerent and threatening.

She scanned the crowd around them but didn't see her uncle. "Harlan's in here, too?"

"Yeah, he's around somewhere. He's checking out the purebred Charolais bulls in one of the barns. I'm meeting him at the steak house in town for dinner in an hour. Why don't you join us?"

"Thanks, but I can't. I promised some friends I'd have dinner with them tonight," Rachel lied without a single twinge of conscience.

"Take a rain check and join Dad and me instead. We haven't had a chance to talk since the funeral and the reading of the will. Granddad was big on family connections. He'd have wanted us to keep in touch."

Hardly. Rachel didn't say a word out loud but realized too late that her expression must have revealed her thoughts, for Lonnie stiffened and his faint smile disappeared as he glared at her.

"It's late and I have to run," she said quickly. "Nice seeing you."

She turned on her heel, but he caught her arm, holding her in place and bending closer until his face was only inches from hers.

"That crazy horse of yours is going to lose tomorrow and when he does, you'd better trailer him home, turn him out to pasture and cancel your contact with McCloud. You won't like what might happen if you don't."

"Are you threatening me?" she demanded, refusing to let him see how much his grip hurt her arm. She could smell whiskey on his breath and knew alcohol only made him meaner and more reckless.

"No, of course not. That would be illegal." He grinned, a brief baring of his teeth. "Just giving you a little advice, cousin. For your own good."

He let go of her and walked past, purposely bumping her with his shoulder as he went. Absently rubbing her aching arm, she watched him until he was out of sight, swallowed up by the shifting throng.

Lonnie was as much a bully as his father, she thought, but he was more of a loose cannon. While Harlan was likely to use money and influence to get his way, Lonnie wasn't beyond using physical force. She hadn't expected him to openly make threats, however, and wished she had taken up Charlie or her mother's offer to share the two-hour drive and overnight stay to watch Ransom's first race. Lonnie might bully her when she was alone, but it was unlikely he would have done so if Charlie or Judith were present.

She left the midway behind and crossed the parking field and highway to the motel, closing her eyes and sighing with pleasure when she stepped inside the air-conditioned room. The crowd noise and carnival music outside were muted by the walls and the quiet chatter of a DJ coming from the small radio she'd turned on earlier.

She walked into the bathroom, stripping off jeans and blouse as she went. The mirror over the vanity revealed red finger marks on her arm where Lonnie had grabbed her, and Rachel frowned with annoyance, knowing they'd turn blue and bruised by tomorrow.

Thirty minutes later she'd showered, changed into clean jeans and a white tank top, pulled her hair up into a ponytail and applied light makeup.

Hours had passed since she'd stopped for a sandwich and a salad at a highway truck stop, and she was more than ready for dinner. She slipped her feet into leather sandals, caught up her purse and left the motel room to walk a few blocks to downtown.

The six blocks of Canyon City's central district

had several restaurants. Rachel picked a small cafe that looked appealing, located at the opposite end of town from the steak house. She wanted to be as far away from Lonnie and Harlan as possible. Much to her surprise, she found friends from Wolf Creek seated around a large table. One of the couples was Mack McGonagle and his fiancée Cheryl Plunkett. Rachel was delighted to accept their invitation to join the merry group. After dinner they all walked back to the fairgrounds to stroll up and down the midway. At ten o'clock Rachel said goodnight and left them buying tickets at the Whirling Octopus ride while she headed for the horse barn.

The barn was quiet inside, the stillness broken only by the night sounds of horses shifting on straw and the muted conversations of a scattering of people. Luke was sitting on a bale of hay outside Ransom's stall, braiding strips of leather in a complicated pattern. He looked up as she neared.

"Hi," she said softly, looking past him to check on Ransom. Much to her surprise, a man was inside the stall with Ransom and Daisy. He stood at the manger, breaking up a large flake of hay into smaller pieces. He glanced over his shoulder, saw her and turned back to his work. Rachel's eyes widened and her gaze flew to Luke's face.

"Chase drove down to watch the race tomorrow,"

Luke commented, correctly reading her expression. "I want someone with Ransom at all times. Chase will spell me and David while we eat and sleep."

"Oh, I see." Rachel nodded but she didn't see at all. Chase McCloud was feeding and helping with her horse. It seemed impossible. The brothers must be very close if he'd agreed to look after a horse owned by a Kerrigan. "Ransom's okay?"

"He's fine." Luke's eyes narrowed. "Why are you worried about him?"

"I'm not," she promptly denied before she sighed. "That's not entirely true. I ran into Lonnie earlier. Evidently Harlan's here, too, and they've both made it very clear that they don't want Ransom to race."

Chase lifted his head at her words. He dropped the last chunk of hay into the manger and stepped out of the stall, latching the gate behind him.

Luke rose to his feet, joining Chase. Side by side, the two brothers presented a united front that Rachel suspected was an automatic and unconscious aligning.

"They threatened Ransom? What did they say?"

"Nothing specific. In fact, both of them pretty much said the same thing—that I wouldn't like the consequences if I didn't cancel my contract with you to train Ransom. Neither of them actually threatened to harm Ransom, but I don't trust them, especially Lonnie."

"Smart woman. Are you staying at the Sunset tonight?"

"Yes." Rachel nodded, wondering why he'd asked. The two men stood shoulder to shoulder, their grim expressions every bit as intimidating as their sheer size. An aura of danger surrounded them.

Luke looked at Chase. "Do you want to stay here or take Rachel to the motel?"

"You go to the motel. I'll stay with Ransom. With luck, Lonnie will come looking for him." Chase lifted an eyebrow, a small smile of anticipation curving his mouth.

Luke nodded. "David's already in our room at the motel. I'll walk Rachel over there and be back in fifteen minutes, maybe less."

"Stay there," Chase advised. "Other trainers are spending the night here in the barn, and if I need any help, all I have to do is yell. And if Lonnie or Harlan try to harass Rachel tonight, you can get to her faster from the motel room than the cops can from wherever they are."

"All right. I'll see you early in the morning, probably around 4:30 or 5:00." He took Rachel's elbow and turned her in the direction of the exit.

His hand was warm, the calluses on palm and fingers slightly rough against her bare skin. The mere touch of his hand made her breathing shorten.

"I don't think Lonnie or Harlan will actually harm me, Luke. They're both bullies but I don't believe it's likely they'd follow through. It's Ransom I'm worried about."

"Chase will take care of Ransom. And you have more faith in Lonnie and Harlan than I do. They threatened you because I'm training your horse—that makes you my responsibility, at least until you're home safe in Wolf Creek again."

"Oh." Rachel felt a spark of gratitude for his consideration but the prospect of walking with Luke through the sultry evening darkness sent a shiver of anticipation and trepidation up her spine. She fell into step beside him, and his hand dropped from her arm, leaving its warm imprint against her skin.

They left the midway and wound their way past a tangle of cables and cords behind the Sno-Cone vendor, circled around a semitrailer stamped with the carnival's logo, and finally reached the trampled grass and dirt lanes that divided the uneven rows of trailers, cars and trucks.

Neither Luke nor Rachel spoke until they reached the motel. She unlocked her door, pushed it open and reached inside to switch on the wall lamp before turning to look at him.

"Thanks for walking with me." She glanced at the darkened rooms on either side of her own. The only lighted windows were in the offices at the far end of the single-story motel. "I hadn't realized how dark it would be."

"No problem. I'm in room thirty-five. If you need me during the night, just call."

"I'm sure I'll be fine but it's very good to know I'm not alone. Thanks so much."

His gaze left hers, dropped to her mouth, then lifted to meet hers again. Rachel caught her breath at the searing heat in his eyes. "How grateful are you?" His voice was deeper.

Rachel thought about the empty bed behind her, the man in front of her, and wondered what the cost of kissing him would be. "How grateful do you think I should be?"

His mouth curved in a slow smile that sent her pulse rocketing. "You could ask me in and give me a tour of your room."

"I don't think so." She shook her head, trying to fight the certain knowledge that he wanted this as badly as she did.

"If you're worried about tomorrow, we can agree that what happens here tonight, in the dark, stays in the dark. I won't remind you in the morning."

"Promise?"

He nodded but he didn't reach for her. Instead, he continued to wait. Emboldened by his restraint,

Rachel curved her hands over the slope of his shoulders and leaned toward him. She hesitated a breath away from his lips. The heat in his expression seared her, the muscles beneath her palms tight with control.

She brushed her lips against his, once, twice. His mouth was warm and held the faint flavor of coffee. Reassured by his control, Rachel lifted her hands from his shoulders to his cheeks and cupped his face as her mouth settled on his.

Luke gripped her waist, steadying her, but he didn't gather her closer even though she could feel the tension in his arms. He let her set the pace, and Rachel was soon lost, drunk on the slow kiss that quickly had her body burning, swelling her breasts and melting her reservations like hot wax. When she licked his bottom lip, he growled and wrapped his arms around her, nearly lifting her off her feet as he ravaged her mouth.

When he eased his mouth from hers and lifted his head at last, Rachel was disoriented and breathing hard, her balance unsteady when he set her back on the step.

"Are you sure you don't want to ask me in?" His voice rasped, husky with arousal.

Rachel shuddered and braced herself on the doorknob behind her. "No," she managed to get out. "I don't think so."

He touched the brim of his hat and stepped back. "Go inside and lock the door."

"Luke…" Rachel said impulsively, giving in to the need that pulsed through her body.

He looked at her without speaking.

Sanity returned and she searched for something less dangerous to say. "I'd like to watch David ride Ransom in the morning."

He shrugged. "He'll be on the track at five."

"Thanks."

"You don't have to thank me. Ransom's your horse."

"Right." Rachel nodded. "I'll see you in the morning, then."

She stepped over the threshold, closing and locking the door before leaning against it, her legs weak, her breathing still too fast.

I've got to stop giving in to temptation. I shouldn't have kissed him, she thought. Luke thought they should go to bed together and burn away the desire that blazed between them. He seemed to think it was like a craving for chocolate and if they indulged and sated themselves, the raging need would disappear.

But I don't think this is going to go away, she thought. *It's as strong—no, stronger—than it was after he kissed me the first time.* She groaned and pushed away from the door, muttering aloud, lecturing herself about her lapse in good sense as she undressed and climbed into bed.

Chapter Eight

Dew lay on the grass and the sun still hid below the horizon when Rachel left her motel room the next morning. The little town of Canyon City nestled in a broad valley with mountain peaks lining the eastern horizon. At this altitude, the hot summer days gave way to cool evenings that in turn became chilly dawns. By ten, the thermometer would register in the upper seventies, well on its way to midafternoon temps in the lower nineties, but for now the cool air required warmer clothing than summer shorts and sandals.

Rachel tugged her zipper pull higher and tucked her chin into the folds of the blue hooded sweatshirt she wore over jeans and a T-shirt. Tennis shoes and socks kept her feet dry as she walked through the wet grass.

The small carnival was silent, locked down and deserted in the predawn, but the horse barn was busy with owners and riders preparing their mounts for early-morning exercise.

Luke was inside the stall with Chase, watching David buckle a halter on Daisy. Ransom was already saddled and bridled, shifting restlessly in the deep bedding straw. David looked up and nodded at her.

"Good morning, Rachel."

"Hi, David." She leaned on the closed stall door. "How's Ransom this morning?"

"He's a little wired," Luke answered.

"Did you have any visitors last night, Chase?"

He shook his head. "None."

"Thank goodness." Rachel breathed a sigh of relief. "Thanks for staying with him."

"No problem."

"Is Daisy going out on the track with Ransom?" she asked Luke.

"Yes. As a matter of fact, why don't you lead her. Chase, David and I will bring Ransom."

"Of course." Rachel unlatched the door.

"How close are the nearest people?" he said before she swung it open.

Rachel looked over her shoulder, twisting to

check the length of the barn aisle. "There's a horse and rider at the other end of the barn and two people standing outside a stall halfway to the far door. Other than that, everyone seems to be inside with the horses."

"Good." Luke nodded. "Let's take him out."

Rachel swung the gate wide, and Ransom snorted, tugging on the reins and backing up.

"Easy, boy," Luke crooned. "Lead Daisy out, Rachel."

David handed her the nylon lead rope snapped to Daisy's halter and she pulled gently. The little mule stepped out of the stall, eyes bright, expression inquisitive as she moved down the aisle toward the wide doors standing open at the end of the barn.

Rachel turned to walk sideways so she could watch the three men with Ransom. He left the stall in a burst of energy with Luke holding the lead rope, Chase and David behind him. Though he sidled and chewed the bit, his ears swiveling with each new sound, he behaved himself until they were outside. Then someone slammed a gate in the barn, shattering the morning quiet.

Ransom spooked, nearly hauling Luke off his feet as he snorted his displeasure and fear. It was a good ten minutes before he calmed and they resumed their walk to the track. This time, Daisy trotted beside him. Her placid acceptance of the strange surroundings seemed to reassure him, although he still jumped at each new noise.

A small John Deere tractor chugged by, pulling a farm disc used to smooth the dirt track surface, and Ransom reared, eyes wide with fear although the rattling machinery was yards away.

Again, Luke quieted him and after several minutes, had him moving forward again. At last, they reached the rail of the oval track and Rachel sighed with relief. Luke and David walked Ransom through the gate while Rachel tied Daisy's lead rope to the white-painted rail. Chase halted nearby, folding his arms across his chest to watch silently.

David listened carefully, head bent, while Luke gave him last-minute instructions. Then he nodded and Luke gave him a leg up into the saddle. Ransom settled down, calmer now with David on his back, and Luke joined Rachel at the fence.

"Did you sleep well last night?"

Rachel glanced sideways. At least two feet of open space separated them, and his hands were safely tucked into the pockets of the faded denim jacket he wore unsnapped over a black T-shirt and jeans. Nevertheless, she felt the brush of his gaze as it moved over her face, dropping to her mouth and lingering before returning to her eyes. He arched a brow and she realized she'd been standing silently, staring at him.

"Yes, I did. Did you?"

"I managed to get to sleep around midnight. After I took a cold shower."

Heat moved up her throat and flooded her cheeks. She looked beyond him at Chase, several feet away and apparently not listening to their conversation. "I thought you promised last night that we wouldn't talk about this," she murmured.

He smiled, a slow, crooked grin that flashed white teeth and made her yearn. "All I said was I took a cold shower and went to sleep. What's wrong with that?"

"You're incorrigible. And I refuse to discuss this." She turned her head to watch David walk Ransom away from them down the track. "Ransom seems calmer."

"He likes David." Luke seemed willing to let the subject of late-night kisses drop, at least for now. He folded his arms across his chest, adopting the same pose as Chase, his gaze focused on horse and rider. For the moment, they had the track to themselves. "But he's still unpredictable. It's hard to say how he'll react in unfamiliar surroundings."

David urged Ransom into a lope, then let him move easily around the track. The stallion didn't appear to fight him, obeying his commands.

"David's going to take him around a couple of times and let him get used to the place. He'll break him out the second time he reaches us," Luke explained when horse and rider were on the far side of the oval.

Rachel nodded, holding her breath as Ransom cantered nearer, then moved past the rail where they stood to begin his second lap. When they reached the far side again, both she and Luke pulled stopwatches from their pockets.

Ransom drew even with the rail where Rachel stood with Luke and Chase. David bent forward, whispering in the stallion's ear as he loosened the reins. Ransom broke into a run, David low over his neck as they raced around the track. Horse and rider were a blur of movement as they rounded the final turn and flew past the three standing at the rail.

Rachel looked at her stop watch and her eyes widened.

"Did you get the same time I did?" She asked Luke, holding out her watch so he could read the numbers.

"Oh, yeah." He grinned broadly, elated, and turned his palm so she could see his watch face.

"Wow," she breathed, stunned.

"That pretty much sums it up." Luke tucked the silver watch into his jeans pocket. "He's fast. No doubt about it."

"But is he fast enough?"

"On a track with no other horses, no gate to leave from, no starter's gun to deal with, and no crowd noise he is," Luke confirmed. "Whether the same will hold true when the actual race starts remains to be seen."

Rachel crossed her fingers and prayed. But Ransom's good behavior during his early-morning run didn't transmit to the race that afternoon. He spooked when the starter's gun went off, rearing and bucking. David managed to settle him and get him to circle the track, but he came in dead last, despite turning in an excellent time.

She walked back to the barn with David and Daisy, Luke and Chase keeping Ransom on a tight lead ahead of them. They took a route to the rear of the barn that avoided crowds. Ransom could still hear the noise of people, however, and he danced and sidled, chewing the bit, sweat darkening his coat.

Rachel waited with Daisy outside the stall while the men removed his tack and rubbed him down.

"He did so well this morning when you worked him," she said. "I was really hoping he'd behave himself this afternoon."

"This was his first real race," David said. "He's going to kick butt next time, aren't you, boy?" A curry brush in each hand, he swept long strokes over the sweat-dampened hide where the saddle had been. Ransom swung his head in response to David's voice and shifted from one side to the other, still visibly agitated, although he was much calmer now that he couldn't hear the crowds.

"Do you think he'll be better next time?"

Luke shrugged. "Hard to tell. The real problem is the starting gates. He hates being enclosed in a small space. I tried him in the small three-horse gate at home and he never really accepted it, although he finally stopped trying to climb over the top to get out."

Rachel's hope that Ransom would win races sooner, rather than later, wavered. "Will he grow accustomed to the gate?"

"I sure as hell hope so," Luke said. "If he doesn't, he'll never win a big race."

"And that's the goal," she murmured.

"That's the goal," he agreed.

Rachel fell silent, watching the two men groom Ransom.

"Hey, Rachel." David broke the comfortable silence. "Are you going to the dance tonight?"

"I hadn't thought about it, are you?"

"Sure."

"He met some local girls at the carnival last night," Luke said dryly.

"That's right." David winked at Rachel. "Poor Luke's too old to dance or he could come along with me and check out the women."

"Old?" Luke threw a curry brush at David but he ducked and it flew past his shoulder before landing on the straw-covered floor. Ransom shifted abruptly and swung his head to eye Luke with alarm. Daisy huffed softly but didn't stop chewing her mouthful of oats. "Keep that up, kid, and I'll have to reconsider setting a curfew for you. Your mom asked me to make sure you were in bed by eight every night."

"She did not!"

"Did too."

"Did not."

Rachel couldn't help but laugh at the rapid-fire exchange as the two argued while Chase watched silently, half smiling. Luke's easy camaraderie with his young cousin gave her a whole new insight into his personality. During his conversations with her, the underlying sexual tension between them made her feel as if their interactions were potential minefields to be carefully negotiated. But with David he was relaxed and easy, and she suspected this was the real Luke, the man his friends and family knew.

This Luke wasn't intimidating. He was charming, and unfortunately for her peace of mind, she found him all the more attractive. She actually liked him.

* * *

The following weekend, Luke entered Ransom in the annual quarter horse race at the local county fair, held just outside Wolf Creek.

Mack McGonagle parked his parent's RV at the fairgrounds and invited Rachel to join the crowd of friends gathering on Saturday night at a campfire.

Dark clouds loomed on the horizon, threatening rain, as Rachel drove from Section Ten to town. Thunder rumbled in the distance when she left her car and walked across the field, thronged with revelers, to join Mack and Cheryl's group.

There were easily a dozen people there, sprawled on the ground or sitting in folding aluminum lawn chairs around the firepit, most of them drinking beer or soda, some of them toasting marshmallows over the flames.

Luke stood on the far side of the fire with Frank O'Brian, a friend from school, talking with a group of men Rachel recognized as horse owners and trainers from the race at Canyon City.

"Come join me," Cheryl called, pulling an empty chair closer to her own as Rachel circled the party to reach her. "Mack and I saw the race this afternoon," Cheryl continued as Rachel sat down. "That horse of yours is fast."

"Yes, but he didn't win," Rachel said wryly.

"True, but just like last week, once he settled down and ran, he was quicker than any other horse on the track."

"But will he ever do that when he's supposed to? That's the question."

"Don't worry, honey." Cheryl patted her arm with sympathy. "You've got the best possible trainer. If anyone can make that horse win, it's Luke."

"Was your horse the one that bucked after the starter's gun went off today?" A woman on the other side of Cheryl leaned forward, joining their conversation with friendly curiosity.

"Yes."

"Rachel, this is Angie Farris—Angie, this is Rachel Kerrigan."

The two exchanged hellos and the three women chatted for a while. Dark clouds gradually obscured the stars, the early evening's balmy temperatures cooling as a breeze picked up. It ruffled Rachel's hair, raising goose bumps on her arms below the short sleeves of her pink cotton top, and carried the scent of rain-washed sage.

Luke moved toward a makeshift drinks table set up on the lowered tailgate of a pickup truck. Mack joined him and they talked for a few moments, then they wandered over to join Cheryl and Rachel. Mack patted his fiancée's shoulder and bent to whisper in her ear.

Luke handed Rachel a steaming mug.

"Thanks." She cradled the hot drink in her palms and smiled up at him, grateful for the gently steaming coffee.

"No problem." His eyes flicked over her and he frowned, running the tip of his forefinger down her arm below the short sleeve. "You're cold." Before she could reply, he shrugged out of his blue plaid shirt and dropped the long-sleeved flannel over her shoulders.

"Oh, thank you." Rachel shivered and pulled the shirt closer. It was still warm from his body and carried his scent. She felt cosseted and unwillingly seduced by his care and concern.

"No problem." He turned away, joining Mack to help him tie down the RV's awning that had begun to snap in the increasing breeze.

A drop of rain landed on Rachel's hand and, seconds later, the fire sizzled as water hit the burning wood.

"Uh-oh." Cheryl stood hastily. "Time to head inside."

Rachel rose with Cheryl, turning to set her cup on the ground before folding her chair.

The rain grew heavier and the two women hurried to store their chairs under the RV.

Rachel hastily said good-night, returned her

empty coffee cup to the box on the tailgate, and was looking around for Luke just as he took her elbow. "There you are. I wanted to return your shirt."

"Keep it on. You're going to get wet. Where did you park?"

"Near the exit—and you're going to get wet, too," she protested, trying to keep up with his long strides as they dodged between two trailers and down the alleyway.

The intermittent raindrops became steadier.

"It's going to pour any minute. We'll never make it to your car without getting soaked." Luke caught her arm and veered to his left, taking her with him as they splashed through puddles. Seconds later he stopped next to a four-wheel-drive truck, yanked open the passenger door, caught Rachel by the waist and lifted her in. "Scoot over."

She slid to the middle of the wide seat and he climbed in beside her, slamming the door after him.

They were just in time. The skies opened up and rain pounded down, thundering on the roof of the cab and turning the windshield opaque.

Luke took off his damp hat and dropped it behind the seat, picking up a small towel he handed to Rachel.

"Thanks." She dabbed water from her face and the ends of her hair, then passed the wet towel to him. Her jeans were spattered with rain, clinging to her legs, and she grimaced at the smear of wetness they made on the buttery-soft leather seat. "Drat, I got your seat wet."

"Don't worry about it." Luke finished wiping raindrops from his face and bare arms and tossed the towel on the floor mat. "This truck has had worse things than rainwater on the seat."

"Like what?" She asked, curious.

"Like oil from greasy parts when we rebuilt Chase's engine last year. And the half a pot of coffee I spilled last month when I didn't tighten the seal on my thermos. Or the time little Rowdy got sick and lost his dinner one night when I gave Jessie a ride home." He raised an eyebrow and gave her a small grin. "Need any more examples?"

"No." Rachel held up her hand, palm out. "That's more than enough. I promise I won't feel guilty."

Luke peered out the windshield. The dirt and grass field of the makeshift parking lot was awash in water as the rain continued to pour down. "We may be stuck here awhile," he commented.

The interior of the truck cab was suddenly over-whelmingly intimate, and Rachel shivered.

"Are you cold?" He didn't wait for her reply but leaned forward and across her to slide the key into the ignition and twist it. The engine rumbled to life, and Luke adjusted a switch to start warm air moving through the cab. "Better?" He turned his head to look at her.

"Yes, much better."

He settled back against the seat, half turning to face her with his back against the door. "Since we'll be here till the rain lets up, suppose you tell me about yourself."

"What?" Startled, she searched his features, but he didn't laugh.

"I'm serious. Do you realize we grew up in the same town but barely know each another?"

"I suppose that's true," Rachel agreed.

"And it occurred to me that you'll feel a lot more comfortable when we wind up in bed together if we get to know each other first."

"You make it sound as if it's inevitable that we'll sleep together." She frowned at him.

"Oh, it's inevitable," he said softly. "Sooner or later you'll agree with me, and when you do, I don't want you waking up the next morning feeling like you're with a stranger. So," he settled his shoulders more comfortably against the door. "You first. Tell me something I don't know about Rachel Kerrigan."

Her frown deepened. She was torn between refusing or satisfying her curiosity about him.

The small silence grew while she considered her options.

"Or—" he shifted away from the door "—we can skip talking and go straight to foreplay. Works for me."

"Wait." Rachel planted a hand against his chest and pushed. He immediately leaned back against the door. "Here's the deal. I tell you something about me, then you tell me something about yourself, agreed?"

He shrugged. "Sure."

She thought for a moment, sifting through possibilities for the most general of comments. "My family lived with Granddad at his ranch while I was growing up but my father died of cancer when I was five. So when I was a little girl, I became very attached to Charlie and my brother, Zach. Charlie taught Zach and me to ride and do math."

"Ride a horse and do math?" Luke smiled. "That's an odd combination."

"Mom wasn't good at either subject. Now you. Tell me something I don't already know."

"I was bit by a rattlesnake when I was ten and almost died."

"Really? Where?"

"On my chest." He pulled his T-shirt free of his jeans and lifted it, pointing to his right side.

Rachel dutifully looked at the small white scar, trying to keep from staring at washboard abs and smooth male skin.

"I see." She managed to get the words out, but just barely, and breathed a sigh, part relief and part regret, when he tucked his shirt into his jeans again. "Uh, my turn…I won a blue ribbon at the county fair when I was ten."

"What for?"

"A school project about the American West."

"A school project? I bet you never got in trouble with the teacher."

"Not very often. But I bet you did."

"Not very often." He smiled and she couldn't help but return it. "Your turn—tell me something else."

The rain beat a tattoo on the roof as the moments slipped away inside the warm truck cab. Rachel was aware of the simmering attraction between them but she was engrossed in the bits of personal information Luke shared. She wondered if he realized how much of himself he was revealing, then thought maybe she was being equally transparent. Mentally shrugging, she decided to just enjoy the shared intimacy free of the adrenaline rush of physical contact.

When Luke's watch alarm buzzed, Rachel glanced at the dashboard clock and gasped.

"Midnight? It can't be. Have we been talking for two hours?"

"Apparently." Luke pushed the off button on his wristwatch and glanced through the window. "And it's not raining as hard."

"Well," Rachel cleared her throat. "I guess I can make it to my car without getting drenched now."

Luke nodded and opened the door, sliding out and waiting for Rachel to join him before shutting the door and taking her arm. They walked quickly across the field, intermittent raindrops still pelting them, until they reached her car. She dug the keys out of her pocket and opened the door.

"You'd better go inside before you get any wetter."

She slipped his shirt off her shoulders and handed it to him. "I don't think it's going to keep you dry since it's already drenched."

He thrust his arms into the blue flannel but left it unbuttoned, a gust of wind billowing the open shirt around his body. The rain dampened his thick hair, slicking it close to his head, and droplets found their way down his face. Lashes, cheeks and mouth were rain-sheened, gleaming in the gold light of the car's dome lamp that shafted from the open door.

"It's late. Wait for me and I'll follow you home."

"You don't need to, Luke. I've driven home at night, in the dark and the rain, a thousand times."

"I'm sure you have, but I'll feel better if you let me follow you. Humor me."

"All right."

He crooked his index finger.

"What?"

"Come here."

"Luke, I don't think…"

"Good, don't think."

His hands settled on her waist and he urged her sideways, just far enough that he could ease the car door shut. The dome light flicked off, throwing them into darkness. Then he leaned into her and lifted her onto her toes as he bent his head to hers.

Once again Rachel was lost, swamped by the aching need that filled her.

He set her back on her feet and opened the car door, the light immediately coming to life.

"It won't take more than a few minutes to get my truck. Wait for me."

She nodded and slid behind the wheel, watching as he walked away from her, his tall form quickly swallowed by the dark night.

Neither one of them had thought to just drive over to her car in his truck. Amused by how distracted they'd both clearly been, Rachel could only shake her head. She brushed her fingertips over her lips, still throbbing from the pressure of his.

What am I going to do about him?

Later, after waving goodbye to Luke as she turned into her lane and he drove on down the highway, she entered her quiet, dark house and went through her usual bedtime routine on autopilot. When she finally climbed into bed and turned out the light, she lay awake, staring at the ceiling.

I wonder if what happens in the rain, stays in the rain, she thought. She knew she was playing with fire, and every alarm she had was shrieking a warning. The likelihood that she would give in and wind up in bed with him sometime soon was growing with each hot goodnight kiss.

Despite her misgivings, she knew herself well enough to believe hormones alone wouldn't lure her into Luke's bed. She'd never indulged in casual sex and she didn't plan to start.

Although, she confessed to the dark ceiling, *if I were ever tempted, Luke just might be the one guy that could convince me.*

The one consolation was that he seemed willing so far to settle for kisses and hadn't pushed for more. Whether she had the strength of will to refuse him if he did push, was another story. And someday he would—he'd said it was inevitable that they'd go to bed together.

She refused to think why she was questioning

whether she'd turn him down if and when he asked her again for more than steamy kisses.

Because she couldn't sleep with him. He wanted sex from her, and if that's all he ever wanted, heartbreak was a guarantee. Given their family history, she could see no happy outcome for her.

Great, just great. Disgruntled, she turned on her stomach and punched her pillow to tuck it under her cheek. I'm not an innocent blushing virgin. Why can't I just enjoy great sex with the first guy who's really turned me on?

Maybe her girlfriends in Helena were right, she thought gloomily. Maybe she did make too much out of the whole "Is it sex or is it love?" thing.

Chapter Nine

Two weeks before the Denver Sweepstakes, Luke called to confirm Ransom would be entered. Rachel hung up the phone and immediately dialed her mother's number, waiting patiently while it rang twice, three, four times before Judith picked up.

She spent a few moments chatting with her mother about the failure of Judith's latest attempt to convince Zach's boss to give her contact information, before getting to the purpose of the call. "The Denver Sweepstakes is only two weeks away and I wanted to check to make sure we have enough money to pay the entry fee."

"How much is it?"

Rachel quoted the amount Luke had told her.

"That might be a problem." Judith's voice was troubled. "Give me a moment while I total my personal account and add it to the available balance in my brokerage account."

Rachel heard a clatter as Judith put the phone on the desk. She'd already cashed in her own investments, even her 401k was gone. If her mother's accounts didn't cover the Denver entry fee, she had only one option left.

"I added every penny I could." Judith's voice sounded in Rachel's ear. "Sorry, honey, but even if I empty my personal account, we're still short."

Rachel drew a deep breath. She couldn't explain to her mother what she had to do now. "Don't worry, Mom." She was glad her mother couldn't see her face. Judith had always been able to tell when she was lying, even a little white lie. "I have some alternatives."

"Like what? Do you still have some of Gran's inheritance left?"

"No." Rachel wished she had, but she'd invested the small legacy from her grandmother in a mutual fund and she'd sold it two months ago. "But I may be able to swing a loan."

Rachel rang off and sat for a moment, contemplating her plan. She'd hoped against hope she wouldn't have to attempt it, but she could see no other choice.

You could ask Luke to lend you the money. Rachel immediately rejected the small, tempting voice in her head. Their relationship was complicated. She suspected he might agree, but if he did, what then? If they ever did make love, he'd always wonder if she was doing it because she was indebted to him.

No, she couldn't ask Luke.

She glanced at the calendar hanging on the kitchen wall next to the telephone. The coming weekend was circled in red and she'd written the words "Keller Suicide Run" inside the square for Saturday.

She and Ajax had been training just in case they had to earn Ransom's fee for Denver by winning the Suicide Run. Apparently, entering that race was now a necessary part of the plan.

Rachel didn't lie to her mother. Not exactly. But she waited until Judith left to spend the weekend with a longtime girl friend in Billings before leaving for Keller. She didn't want to explain why she was taking Ajax and leaving town on Friday morning.

She was sure Judith would forbid her to enter the Keller Suicide Run if she knew her plans. The race was infamous for the number of riders who ended up with broken bones. She doubted her mother would accept the rationale that Ajax, on whom Zach had once finished first, would keep her safe. But Rachel was counting on Ajax's sheer power and stubborn will to win again. The winner's purse would more than cover Ransom's entry fee in Denver.

She pulled into the truck stop just west of Wolf Creek and was filling the tank of the pickup she'd borrowed from Charlie when Chase drove in and parked at the gas pump beside her.

Rachel nodded and said hello. Chase touched the brim of his Stetson in greeting, and she turned to scan the horse trailer she'd hitched to the truck. Both belonged to Charlie, and inside the trailer, Ajax stood calmly, his nose against the small side opening nearest her.

"I talked to Luke last week. He said Ransom was doing well."

Chase's deep voice startled Rachel. Her hand jerked, bumping the heavy rubber gas hose against the truck fender. She looked over her shoulder and found Chase watching her, one hand holding a gas nozzle, the other resting on the top edge of the bedliner of his big dual-wheeled pickup.

"Um, yes, he is." The sharp smell of gasoline filled the air and she realized she'd spilled fuel down the side of the fender and over her fingers. She pulled a tissue from her jeans pocket and wiped off her hand, wrinkling her nose as the odor lessened but didn't go away.

"You're entering Ransom in the Denver Sweepstakes?"

"That's right." She thought their brief exchange was over but his gaze flicked to the horse trailer hitched to her truck.

"Luke didn't mention you were having him train a second horse."

"I'm not, Luke's only training Ransom. I'm taking Ajax to Keller."

"Keller?" Chase looked puzzled, then his brow cleared. "The Stampede? I didn't realize there were quarter horse races in Keller this year."

"There aren't."

Chase's features were polite but Rachel could almost hear the swift whirr of his brain as he figured why she could be taking Ajax to Keller. She wished she hadn't said so much.

He waited, clearly expecting her to comment further. When she didn't, he merely nodded politely. "Good luck."

"Thanks." The gas clicked off. Relieved, Rachel quickly returned the nozzle to the pump, replaced her truck's fuel cap and hurried inside to pay the attendant. She passed Chase in the doorway just as she was exiting, but since there were two people walking behind her, she could only nod farewell.

Chase was still inside the truck stop when she started the engine and eased the truck and trailer out onto the highway.

"Thank goodness," she murmured with relief as the truck stop disappeared from her rearview mirror. She'd been caught off guard when he spoke to her, and instead of evading his questions she'd blurted out the truth. Or enough of the truth that he'd probably guessed her plans for Ajax.

"Ugh." She groaned aloud. But it probably made little difference, she decided. What was the likelihood of Chase McCloud caring if she was going to the Keller Stampede, let alone telling anyone? Zero to none.

If she failed, no one would be the wiser. If she succeeded, she'd have the money for Ransom's entry fee in Denver.

Either way, she and Ajax were committed to entering the Suicide Run at the Keller Stampede.

Chase tucked his change into his jeans pocket as he walked back to his truck. He pulled open the driver's side door of the cab and paused, staring speculatively down the highway where Rachel Kerrigan's vehicle had disappeared only moments before.

Why would she be taking a horse to the Stampede? The only possible reason he could think of didn't make sense.

He climbed into the cab and leaned across the seat to take a cell phone from the glove compartment. He dialed a familiar number, then started the engine and pulled forward to park just to the right of the exit, the diesel engine rumbling as it idled.

Luke was stepping out of the shower when his cell phone rang. He picked it up off the counter and punched the On button. "Yeah?"

"Hey, Luke."

"Chase."

"I thought you might like to know that I'm sitting at the truck stop."

Luke rubbed the towel over his wet hair and wondered what his brother was up to. It wasn't like Chase to telephone mid-morning just to chat. On the other hand, if there was a genuine emergency in the family, Chase wouldn't have bothered saying hello, he would have bluntly told him the bad news, no matter how serious. "And you're just checking in to tell me you bought gas?"

"More to tell you who else was pumping gas."

"Okay, I'll bite. Who?"

"Rachel Kerrigan."

"Yeah?" Luke wondered what his brother was up to but decided to play along.

"Yup, she pulled out a few minutes ago, heading west. She's on her way to Keller."

"Keller?" Luke frowned. "Why the hell is she going there?"

"To the Keller Stampede. And she had her brother's big Appy gelding in the trailer."

Luke frowned at the wall. "Did she say what she was doing in Keller?"

"No. But the Suicide Run is this weekend."

"Shit." Luke was afraid he knew exactly what Rachel was doing. "She wouldn't be that stupid."

"Gossip says she's broke. Is there any reason she'd want to risk her neck—does she need money?"

"Ransom's entry fee for Denver." Luke cursed and slammed his fist on the counter. "Why the hell didn't she just ask me for a loan?"

"I thought she was the one paying you, little brother." Chase's voice was mild. "You giving her money now?"

"If she needed it, yes." Luke said curtly.

"Hmm." Chase's voice was neutral. "How good a rider is she?"

"Hell, I don't know—but she's been living in the city for the last few years. Even hardened riders don't stand a good chance of surviving that crazy race."

"So, what do you want to do about it?"

Luke thought swiftly. "What are you doing for the next few days?"

"What have you got in mind?"

"Will you go to Keller with me?"

"I could do that," Chase said slowly. "But you'll owe me."

"Don't I always?"

"One way or the other," Chase said mildly before the phone went dead in Luke's ear.

Luke tossed the phone on the bed and yanked on his shorts and jeans, pulling a T-shirt over his head before he sat and tugged his boots on. Mentally ticking off the dozen things he needed to do before he turned Ransom over to David, he paused only to throw some clothes into a bag.

Within the hour, he and Chase were on the road, his rawboned quarter horse-Appy mix named Noah in the horse trailer behind them.

If Rachel was planning what he thought, he'd do whatever was necessary to stop her. The Suicide Run was a wild, free-for-all event on a bluff above a river. Riders were bunched in a pack and at the starting gun, galloped to the edge where they went over and down a nearly 90 degree cliff. A few short yards from the base of the bluff, horse and rider had to swim across a river before racing another quarter mile to the finish line.

The melée was no-holds-barred chaos. Luke had entered three times in his early twenties and won twice. He knew how rough the ride was and there was no way he was letting Rachel enter and risk injury.

Luke and Chase drove straight through, stopping only for gas and strong coffee, and arrived in the small town of Keller late in the afternoon. They registered at a motel before driving to the outskirts of town where the stampede grounds were located.

After a quick survey of the campground beside the river confirmed Rachel wasn't there, Luke picked a parking spot with a clear view of the entrance gate. Then he unloaded Noah, bought a burger and coffee from a fair vendor and settled down to wait while Chase left to settle Noah into his assigned stall at the barn in.

An hour later Luke slumped in the truck cab, legs stretched out, arm resting on the rolled-down window, hat tipped over his eyes while he tried to stay awake. He'd caught himself nodding off more than once and was considering a trip for more coffee when a blue Ford truck and horse trailer slowed, turned off the highway and drove into the campground.

Luke sat up, eyes narrowed as the truck drew closer and he recognized Rachel behind the wheel. The surge of relief he felt was erased by the anger that simmered just below the surface. Rachel pulled into a slot two alleyways over; Luke shoved open his truck door, stepped out, slammed the door behind him and strode toward her.

The drive from Wolf Creek to Keller was nearly the width of the state. Rachel was tired and stiff as she left the truck cab and walked to the back of the trailer to let Ajax out for fresh grass and water.

He whickered at her through the slats as she passed.

"Hey, boy." Rachel trailed her fingers along the side of the trailer on her way to the gate. "I bet you'll be glad to get out of there, won't you."

She reached for the latch and started to slide it free when a hand closed over her shoulder.

Startled, she spun around. Luke stood not two feet away, and Rachel stared at him in shock. "What are you doing here?"

"I heard you were heading to Keller. The better question is, why?"

He knows. "Who told you?"

"I talked to Chase. He mentioned he ran into you at the truck stop in Wolf Creek."

"What a small world."

"Yeah, isn't it." A muscle flexed in Luke's jaw, his eyes narrowed. "You didn't answer my question— what are you doing here? And why did you bring him?" He jerked his chin at the trailer behind her.

She looked over her shoulder at Ajax. The big gelding's black muzzle was visible as he sniffed inquisitively through the gap in the slats. "You mean Ajax?" She squared her shoulders. "I'm entering him in the Suicide Run."

"The hell you are."

"Oh, yes I am." Her voice was calm, perfectly level.

"Are you nuts? Have you any idea how many people break bones in that race?"

"I'm well aware of the statistics. But I've got Ajax. He belongs to Zach, and my brother was riding him when he won the race five years ago."

"So what? That was your brother, not you."

"Zach won on Ajax after he was wounded in Afghanistan and went through months of physical therapy in Helena. My brother's good, but he swore Ajax was responsible for winning that race. And with him, I can win, too."

Luke yanked his hat from his head and slapped it against his thigh in frustration. "You are so bloody stubborn. Zach Kerrigan was always a hell of a rider.

Are you telling me you can ride as well as him—especially after spending the last few years living in a city apartment? Did you ride every day while you were in Helena?"

"No, I didn't. I couldn't," Rachel conceded. "But I've ridden Ajax every day of the last two-plus months since I came home. I can do this. I have to," she added.

"No, you don't have to," Luke growled. "Chase and I trailered my Appy with us. I'll ride Noah and take your place."

"I can't let you do that." Rachel shook her head. "This is my problem, not yours, and I'll take care of it."

"And risk breaking your neck? I don't think so." When she only eyed him stubbornly and didn't give in, Luke tried another tack. "I've entered the Suicide Run three times and won twice. I know what I'm doing, Rachel. And so does Noah."

Rachel sighed. "I can't ask you to do this for me, Luke. If anything happened to you, it would be my fault."

"You're not asking me to do it. In fact, you're being pretty damned insistent about me *not* doing it." He looked away from her, the tension growing before he spoke again. "I'll loan you the money. How much do you need?"

Rachel flushed but pride kept her voice steady. "No. I won't borrow from you."

"Well that sounds pretty definite."

"I'm sorry." She raked her hands through her hair, pushing it back over her shoulders. "I'm trying to keep the business between us separate from the…" She paused, searching for the right word to describe what they had. Were they having an affair? Could it be called a relationship? She didn't know. In fact, she didn't have a clue what he thought lay between them. Did he feel anything beyond the physical connection? Sometimes she thought he did. Then, at other times, she wasn't sure.

"Personal?" Luke prompted her when she remained silent. "You want the business between us totally divided from any personal connection? Is that what you're trying to say?"

"Yes. If I accept money from you, how will you ever know if I have ulterior motives?"

He laughed, a short, incredulous sound. "You've got to be kidding. In the first place, you've never asked me for money. In the second place, neither one of us could fake what happens when we touch each other."

"You think so?" Did he feel what she felt when she was with him? Did he share the sensation of being caught up in a force more powerful than a hurricane, of being burned alive by the passion that raged between them.

"I know so."

Rachel shivered at the conviction in his words and the intensity of his gaze.

"Now that's settled, will you cancel your entry and let me compete with Noah in your place?"

"No."

"Dammit, Rachel."

Frustration poured off him in waves. Rachel was torn, even though she saw no way to make them both happy. "Please try to understand, Luke. It's not that I think I can ride better or that I have more chance of winning, because I know I don't. It's the principle."

"You mean it's the damned feud between our families." He nearly snarled the words, his eyes hot.

Rachel nodded. "Partly, yes." She ignored the curse he growled, intent on making him understand. "We haven't talked about the feud, and I confess I've purposely avoided the subject. But just because we don't discuss it, doesn't mean it's gone away. Sooner or later, we'll have to deal with our families. I don't want to do anything to give your family cause to think ill of me. Or of you, either."

"I don't answer to my family."

"I know. But I can't believe they were happy when they heard we'd be working together. I don't want to create any more dissension in your life than I already have."

"They'll have to get used to it sometime."

"What do you mean?" She searched his features.

"I mean that when we finish at Denver and go home to Wolf Creek, I'm not going to stop seeing you."

Rachel's heart leaped with delight before reason returned. "It won't work, Luke."

"We'll make it work. Our families will have to adjust."

"How?" She spread her hands in frustration. "How can we possibly make this work when everyone in both our lives forbids it? Are you willing to break your mother's heart? Your father's heart? How can we do this?"

He caught her hands in his and pulled her closer until her breasts touched his chest. "I don't know how we'll do this, but we will."

Rachel stared up at him. His eyes were fierce, the blue turned dark. "I don't see how…" she whispered.

He stopped her by placing his forefinger over her lips. "We'll work it out."

"I just don't see…"

Luke bent his head and covered her mouth with his, silencing her with a brief, hard kiss. "We'll work it out. Trust me."

"Hey, Luke."

Rachel looked over Luke's shoulder. Chase McCloud walked toward them, Stetson shading his eyes from the hot sunlight, his expression unreadable.

He nodded at Rachel in greeting and gestured at the steep bluff beyond the river. "I thought you might want to take a look at the condition of the run."

"Not a bad idea." Luke glanced down at Rachel. "If you want to check in and register, I'll unload your horse and let him graze while we're waiting."

"Thanks." Rachel glanced around. "Which way is the office?"

Luke pointed to the left. "Just past the 4-H cattle barn and across from the carnival."

"I'll be back as soon as possible—thanks for taking care of Ajax."

"No problem."

Luke and Chase watched Rachel walk away, her slim figure quickly disappearing among the people thronging the field and midway.

"Did she agree to let you ride Noah in her place?"

"No."

Chase glanced sideways at him. "No? Then why don't you just loan her the money?"

"I offered. She refused."

Chase's eyes narrowed in consideration. "Well, I'll be damned. Did she say why?"

"Oh, yeah," Luke said in disgust. "She's got some

half-baked idea that if she accepts a loan, my family will believe she took advantage of me."

"She's worried about taking advantage of you? That's a switch."

"What do you mean by that?" Luke snarled.

"Whoa." Chase held up his hands. "Nothing, nothing. I'd have bet money on the likelihood of *you* taking advantage of *her*, that's all. You look at her like she's a New York steak and you haven't eaten in a month."

"That's not true."

"Hey, I'm not saying you shouldn't—she's a good-looking woman."

Luke shrugged. He shifted, glancing across the crowded field where Rachel had long since disappeared. "You don't mind?"

"Mind? Why would I mind?"

"Because she's a Kerrigan."

Chase was silent for a moment. "Are you sleeping with her?"

"That's none of your business."

"No, it's not. And if that's all you're doing, I have to ask myself why you'd wonder if I cared."

Luke met Chase's gaze but couldn't read anything but mild curiosity. "I just do, that's all."

Chase was silent for a long moment. "Remember what Granddad said about Kerrigan women?"

"He said a lot of things. I don't remember everything he said, especially about the Kerrigans."

"You remember this one. In fact, you quoted him at dinner when you told the family you were going to train Rachel's horse."

"Ah," Luke nodded. "You mean his belief that the Kerrigan women aren't as bad as their men?"

"That's it. Maybe Granddad was right." He gestured at the carnival midway. "I'm going to get a cold drink. You want one?"

"Sure. I'll see you at the barns as soon as Rachel has a stall assigned for Ajax."

"Sounds good."

Luke stared after his brother as he strode away and disappeared in the crowd.

Unless he was mistaken, Chase had just told him he liked Rachel. He wondered briefly if the world had slipped off its axis. He shook his head and turned to walk the few steps to Rachel's horse trailer, mulling over the astounding conversation he'd just had with Chase.

Although, he asked if I was sleeping with her. That doesn't mean he wouldn't care if I was dating her back home. Or if I wanted more.

Luke's hand stilled on the latch of Rachel's horse trailer.

Do I want more? Like what? He knew he didn't

want to stop seeing Rachel after Ransom ran at
Denver. But beyond that, what?

Hell, he thought. *What difference does it make
what I want? More than likely Rachel would choose
her family over me. She'd never do anything to hurt
her mother, and she and Zach are tight.* Regardless
of what either of them wanted, the possibility of a
long-term future together was doubtful.

Shelving the questions for which he had no
answers, Luke slid the latch free and swung open the
gate. When Rachel returned, he was on the far side
of the open field, the lead attached to Ajax's halter
held loosely in his hand while the big horse grazed
contentedly on sun-dried grass.

An hour later, Rachel walked between Luke and
Chase as they left the horse barn and midway behind.
They reached the strip of land that lay between the
Suicide Run's finish line and the river. Very little
grass was left on the wide lane since riders had been
practicing there for several days, churning the grass
and dirt into ankle-deep dust.

They followed the track to the riverbank and
watched as two riders urged their mounts into the
water on the far side.

"It's deeper than I expected," Rachel commented
as the horses reached the middle third of the flow and
were forced to swim.

"Deep enough to drown if a rider falls in the pack," Luke agreed. "The good news is the bottom along this stretch of river is solid and fairly even. Even so, horses lose their footing and go down every year."

"But no horse or rider has actually died, have they?"

"Not recently. Back in the 1930's there were a couple of deaths, and I think one of them was a rider that drowned."

Rachel shivered.

"The ASPCA is always trying to close down the run, but horses rarely get seriously hurt. So far, the local folks responsible for organizing the race have managed to fend them off. But injury to the riders…" Luke shook his head. "That's a different story."

"Luke broke his arm the year he lost," Chase put in.

Alarmed, Rachel's gaze left the swimming horses to look at Luke. "You broke your arm?"

His lips curved in a half smile, his expression exasperated. "That was my own fault. If I'd let Noah do what he wanted, we wouldn't have collided with Jackson." He absentmindedly rubbed his lower right arm.

"Noah's smarter at this kind of racing than you are," Chase agreed dryly. "Even with one arm out of commission, you almost won that year because of him."

"True."

A rebel yell split the air and all three looked up, searching the cliff above the river for the source of the sound just in time to see a horse and rider launch themselves over the edge.

Rachel caught her breath. The man leaned so far back in the saddle that his shoulders nearly brushed the horse's rump, his legs and stirrups stretched out high over his mount's shoulders. Time seemed to slow, horse and rider moving at a snail's pace as the sorrel gelding descended the nearly perpendicular face of the cliff.

For a moment Rachel thought they were going to reach the bottom without falling. But just when she thought all was safe, the man eased his tight hold on the reins and the sorrel's head lowered. A fatal mistake, for the shift in balance sent the horse tumbling to roll the remaining distance to the valley floor.

Rachel gasped, her hand pressed to her throat as a cloud of dust temporarily obscured the two. Then the riderless horse scrambled to his feet, running several yards before he stopped, breathing hard, and looked back at his owner.

Even though the width of the river separated them, Rachel heard the downed rider swearing and cursing before he stood, slapping dirt and grass from his jeans and shirt while he limped toward his mount.

"Man, he got lucky," Chase commented.

"Damned straight," Luke said with feeling. "Why did he let up on the reins?"

"No idea." Chase shook his head with disgust. "Remember that on Saturday and don't be stupid."

"Hell," Luke snorted, affronted. "That's an amateur's mistake. The fool's liable to break his neck tomorrow."

"Either his or his horse's. Or worse yet, he's likely to go down and take half the pack with him," Chase commented.

Relieved that neither horse nor rider appeared to be seriously injured, Rachel eyed the face of the cliff. Over the years the race had worn a wide swathe where neither weeds nor sagebrush grew. The sandy lip was churned deep by horses, the lower two-thirds corduroyed with grooves from the weight carried on sliding hooves. The region had seen more rain than usual over the spring and summer months, which meant the river was deeper and wider, nearly lapping against the base of the slope.

"Is the river's current a factor?" she asked.

"Not if it's a dry year, but this summer…" Luke considered the river and the narrow strip of land dividing it from the bottom of the cliff. "Yeah, this year, it could be a problem."

Rachel shivered, contemplating the increased

risk. Ajax was powerful, but swimming wasn't his strong suit. In fact, he even disliked wading across the narrow creek in his pasture at the ranch.

Luke glanced at his wristwatch. "I know it's early, but I haven't eaten anything except fast food all day. I'd kill for a steak."

"Sounds good to me," Chase replied.

Both men looked expectantly at Rachel.

"Sure, why not?"

No one in Wolf Creek would have believed she could have shared such a companionable dinner with Luke and his brother, she thought later, as the three of them returned to the fairgrounds to check on the horses.

Both Ajax and Noah were veterans of fairground noise and crowds. They stood quietly in their respective stalls, whickering a welcome when their owners joined them. Chase and Luke stepped inside with Noah, and Rachel continued on to Ajax, three stalls farther on down the aisle.

She checked Ajax's hay and water then brushed his already-glossy hide, eyeing the McCloud brothers as they carried on a conversation she couldn't hear. At last Luke nodded decisively and left Noah's stall, his long strides making short work of the space between Noah and Ajax's temporary quarters.

"Are you about finished with him?" Luke unlatched the gate and stepped inside.

"Yes." Rachel gave Ajax a final pat and returned the brush to the bucket of grooming aids.

"Good." Luke took the bucket from her and held open the gate. "Let's go."

Rachel waited until they were outside the barn and walking toward her truck before she spoke. "Let's not argue again about my riding tomorrow, Luke."

He looked at her, his face shadowed by his hat. He didn't speak until they reached his truck.

"Do you have a room in town?"

"No. The motels were full when I got here." She gestured across the crowded parking field in the general direction of Charlie's truck and trailer. "I thought I'd sleep in the trailer and use the campground showers in the morning."

Luke shoved his hand in his jeans pocket and pulled out his truck keys and a room key. "Chase and I are staying with the horses tonight so you can have our room. It's the Vista Motel, a block north of Main Street, just past Smiley's Cafe."

"I can't take your room, Luke," she protested.

"Suit yourself, but it's empty."

"Why are you spending the night in the barn?"

"Because this is the Suicide Run and it's not unheard of for entrants to tamper with other riders' horses. Might not happen, but I don't plan to leave anything to chance."

"I see. In that case…" Rachel took the keys from him and tucked the room key into her jeans pocket. "I'll take you up on your offer."

He nodded, wrapped an arm around her and kissed her, one fierce swift kiss that left her legs trembling, before he stalked off.

He was clearly not happy with her riding tomorrow.

Well, neither am I, Rachel thought as she climbed into the truck and twisted the ignition key. The image of the horse tumbling headfirst down the cliff was burned on her brain. *But I don't have an alternative. This is as good as it gets.*

Chapter Ten

Luke and Chase were standing outside Ajax's stall when Rachel arrived at the barn the following morning. Both men looked equally grim.

"What's wrong?" She looked past them at Ajax but he seemed to be his usual, healthy self.

"Lonnie's here," Luke said.

"Where?" She looked up and down the wide aisle but didn't see her cousin among the shifting crowd that half filled the alleyway.

"He's not in the barn. I watched him drive in about an hour ago and park across the field. He's pulling a horse trailer." A muscle twitched along Luke's jawline.

"He brought a horse? Then he's entering the run?"

"It looks that way." Chase nodded, his face set.

Anger, hot and bright, raced through Rachel. "Damn him. How did he find out I was here?"

"More important, why is he here?" Luke said.

"To annoy me, that's why," Rachel shot back. "He must have found out I need money to continue racing Ransom, so he wants to win the run today."

"I think it's more than that. I don't think he cares if he wins the race. I think he plans to make sure you don't. And the easiest way to do that is to take you out."

"You actually think he'd purposely hurt me?"

"I think he's capable of just about anything." Luke's gaze didn't waver from hers.

Rachel flicked a glance at Chase and found him watching her, his eyes fierce.

"Believe it," he said tersely.

"Great, just great," Rachel muttered. She thrust her hand through her hair, turning to stare down the length of the busy barn. "Now what am I going to do?"

"You're going to scratch Ajax and let me ride in your place."

She shook her head and turned to look at him. "I can't do that. Lonnie knows you're training Ransom. Wouldn't he put two and two together and try to take you out of the race instead of me?"

"He can try." The curl of Luke's mouth and the look in his eyes made the hair rise on her nape.

"I don't know…"

He stepped closer until the toes of their boots touched. "I don't want you hurt."

She refused to give way, which meant she had to tip her head back to meet his stare. "I don't want you hurt, either. Are you going to drop out?"

"No. I'm not backing away from him." He didn't hesitate. "But I'll give you the prize money when I win. Or I'll loan you the money outright and you can walk away from this."

"I can't do that." Frustrated, Rachel glared at him. "Have you any idea what Zach would say if I had to tell him I borrowed the money from you to save his inheritance?" Besides, she thought, she couldn't use Luke again, not in any way. Her conscience was already eating her alive over the half-truths she'd been forced to tell him. When he found out what she'd done by offering him the land instead of cash for his trainer fee—as he would when she confessed after Ransom raced in Denver—he was going to hate her. She refused to give him more reasons to think ill of her.

"Then don't tell him."

"I won't lie to him." *Nor to you. No more lies.*

Luke swore under his breath, exasperation clear

in his tense muscles and thinned lips. "I'm riding Noah. I'm asking you one last time to drop out, for both our sakes."

"No, Luke. We had this conversation yesterday. This is my obligation—I can't let you do this for me."

"All right." Luke nodded grimly. "But if Noah goes down and I break my arm again, you'll be responsible."

"What?" Rachel frowned at him. "Why would I be responsible for your broken bones?"

"Because if you're riding in the pack, I'll be thinking about you and worrying about protecting you from Lonnie. Being distracted can be deadly in this race. Any rider who isn't a hundred percent focused on his horse and on staying alive is likely to get hurt."

"You're saying I'm a distraction?"

"Always. And when you're in danger, even more so."

Rachel bit her lip. His expression was deadly serious. She realized that knowing Luke was riding would distract her, too. She hated to admit it, but he was right.

"For safety reasons, only one of us should enter," he said. "And if you're honest, Rachel, you have to agree I've got a better chance of winning than you do." She opened her mouth to protest but closed it again when Luke added, "Not because I'm a man and you're a woman. You've only been riding consistently this summer, while I've been on a horse daily since I was two years old and Dad threw me up on my first pony. I've also entered and won the run before. I'm familiar with the track and the dynamics of the race itself. It's not just the terrain that makes it dangerous, it's also the attitude of the riders. Some of them will do anything to win, including purposely taking out any horse and rider that gets in their way. Add Lonnie to the equation and it's too damned dangerous."

Rachel was silent for a long moment, weighing her options.

"All right," she said reluctantly. "I'll drop out."

Relief spread over his features, the stern line of his mouth easing.

"But if you get hurt…" she said fiercely.

"I won't." He wrapped his arms around her in a hard hug.

"Smart woman." A deep voice interrupted them.

Luke slung his arm around her shoulders. "Yeah, she's not riding."

"Good." Chase's blue eyes warmed perceptibly. "In that case, she can help us get Noah ready."

Two hours later Rachel stood next to Chase at the bottom of the cliff, on the fairground side of the river.

The crack of the starting gun and the roar of the crowd above them sent Rachel's heart into her throat. Within seconds, horses and riders poured over the lip of the cliff, quickly stirring up dust that nearly obscured the pack. Luke and Noah were in the lead, neck and neck with two other riders while Lonnie was only a few yards behind bunched with the rest of the competitors.

One horse stumbled and went down at the foot of the cliff, and Lonnie surged forward to compete with Luke and another rider for first place. When they plunged into the river, Lonnie purposely swerved into Luke, knocking Noah off stride. But Noah recovered to forge ahead when they reached the deeper water in the center, swimming with powerful strokes. The big Appy lunged up the riverbank, Lonnie's mount on his heels, and Luke urged Noah on as they raced toward the finish line.

Lonnie's big-boned Thoroughbred gained ground as they thundered down the dirt lane but fast though he was, the other horse couldn't catch Noah. He and Luke reached the finish line a half length ahead of the second-place Lonnie.

"He won!" Rachel realized she was gripping Chase's arm, her fingernails digging into hard muscle. "Sorry."

"No problem." He gave her a rare grin, his blue eyes twinkling. "Pretty exciting, eh?"

"Yes, very." Self-conscious, Rachel pushed her hair back from her face and drew a deep, steadying breath. "Thank goodness he wasn't hurt."

They joined the noisy crowd of spectators pouring onto the track to walk to the finish line, and moments later Chase shouldered his way through the mob around Noah. Luke had his back to them, inspecting Noah's foreleg.

"Hey, Luke." Chase's voice drew Luke's attention and he looked over his shoulder, a broad smile brightening his dusty face as he straightened to face them. "Nice riding."

"Very nice riding," Rachel echoed. River water soaked Luke's jeans and splattered his long-sleeved chambray shirt, turning the coating of dust to mud. The sand and dirt on his face was streaked where water had splashed and run in rivulets down his cheeks. She scanned him swiftly, looking for blood, but except for a long scratch on the back of one hand, she couldn't see any major injuries. "No broken bones?"

He grinned, teeth flashing white in his grubby face. "No broken bones." He looked at Chase. "Where's Lonnie?"

Chase scanned the tightly packed throng. "Looks like he's heading for his truck to load his horse."

"Let's go." Luke held out Noah's reins to Rachel.

"Oh, no, you don't." She shook her head and

glared at them. "It's bad enough my cousin is a Neanderthal, but that doesn't mean you two should make it worse. He lost the race and you won, isn't that enough punishment?"

"No." Both Luke and Chase spoke together.

"Please. Let it go, okay?"

The two men exchanged a look of frustration before Luke nodded reluctantly.

Rachel stood with Chase, watching as the race organizers handed a silver belt buckle and a check to Luke.

"Never again," she vowed as she walked back to the barn with the two men, the mud-spattered Noah's reins looped over Luke's forearm. "You're lucky you weren't killed."

"Hey, lighten up." He lifted the buckle and it gleamed in the bright sun. His knuckles were bruised and bloody. "No broken bones, only a few bruises and scrapes."

"Humph." Rachel knew his torso and legs must have more than a few bruises and she had an overwhelming urge to drag him back to the motel room, strip off his clothes and check his body for more damage. She could hardly bear knowing he'd endured such punishment for her. "I'm just thankful you were riding Noah."

"Me, too," Luke agreed with a lopsided smile.

They reached the barn, and Chase slipped Noah's reins off Luke's arm. "Why don't you grab a shower while I rub Noah down and feed him." He glanced at Rachel. "Do you need any help with Ajax?"

"No, thanks." She returned his easy smile and realized with a start that she'd grown comfortable with Chase over the past weeks. No longer would she think of him as scary, for she'd glimpsed the real man beneath the dangerous-seeming outer image.

Around 10 p.m., after celebrating Luke's win with dinner provided for all the entrants by the Suicide Run Committee, Rachel drove Luke's truck back to the motel. Chase and Luke returned to the fairgrounds where Chase planned to leave for home, driving Rachel's truck with Ajax loaded in the trailer behind. Luke would stay overnight at the barn, letting Noah rest before the long drive home to Wolf Creek the following morning.

Rachel turned on the television and flipped through the channels, but none of the programs appealed. She left the TV on CNN and muted the sound while she turned down the bed. But she wasn't sleepy.

I wonder what Luke's doing.

She glanced at the digital clock on the bedside table. Barely eleven o'clock, but still, Chase had probably left for home by now. She couldn't settle down, her nerves still wound much too tightly from the day's events.

On impulse she grabbed her purse from the small table and headed for the door. Outside, the night was clear and bright, the arch of black-velvet sky spangled with glittering stars.

It was a short ten-minute drive back to the fairgrounds. The sound of the band in the dance hall on the far side of the carnival was barely audible inside the horse barn, the light dim, the space shadowy. Rachel moved quietly down the short entry aisle, straw rustling and several horses whinnying softly as she passed. She rounded the corner and turned left down the long section of the L-shaped barn. Noah's stall was nearly at the end of the aisle, and as she drew nearer, she could make out the form of a man sprawled on a hay bale outside the door.

Luke sat slouched with his back against the door, his hat tipped forward over his eyes, arms folded over his chest. He wore a long-sleeved, western-cut shirt that hung open over a white T-shirt, and his long jeans-clad legs were stretched out before him, ankles crossed. He didn't move as she drew near and halted, the toes of her boots nearly touching his.

"Luke?" She whispered, not wanting to startle Noah.

* * *

He pushed his hat brim back with a forefinger and looked up at her. "Rachel? What are you doing here?"

"I couldn't sleep, so I decided to check on Noah."

Luke glanced over his shoulder at the big horse, drowsing inside the darkened stall. "He's fine—tired, but fine." He yawned, scrubbed his palms down his face, uncrossed his ankles and sat up. "Sit down, I'm getting a kink in my neck looking up at you."

Rachel dropped down onto the bale beside him, stretched out her legs and laughed softly.

"What's so funny?"

"You—complaining about getting a neckache from looking up. That's a switch, usually it's the other way around and I'm looking up at you."

"True." He looked sideways at her. "Not now, though. I'm not that much taller than you when we're sitting down."

Rachel narrowed her eyes, measuring his body against hers. "You're still taller. My shoulders only reach your bicep and look how much longer your legs are." She pointed to his boots, once again crossed at the ankle. They stretched many inches past the spot where her smaller, boot-covered feet rested on the hay-strewn concrete floor. "Hold out your hand."

He obliged and she turned it over, measuring her

hand against his much-bigger palm and longer fingers. "See, even your hands are too tall."

Luke laughed, a bass rumble of amusement that had Noah huffing behind them.

"Shh, you'll wake Noah," Rachel scolded.

"Sorry," he whispered. "I've never heard anyone complain my hands were 'too tall.'"

Rachel waved impatiently. "You know what I mean. Tall people take for granted all their advantages and never for a moment consider the problems the rest of us have with height compensation."

"Height compensation?" He stared at her, baffled. "What do you mean by that?"

"I mean standing on chairs to change lightbulbs or to reach the top shelf of the kitchen cupboard."

"Oh, that kind of height compensating." He grinned at her.

"You have no idea how annoying that sort of thing can be on a daily basis."

"I'll take your word for it."

"Hummph." She folded her arms over her chest and frowned at him.

"Promise not to hit me if I tell you something?" he asked.

"Depends on what you tell me."

He leaned closer, his lips brushing her ear. "You're cute when you're annoyed."

"Men." Rachel shook her head. "That's such a cliché."

"Maybe, but it's true. Of course," he added, "you're pretty cute when you're not annoyed, too."

"And you're very charming. Does that line always work with the women you date?"

He pretended to consider. "No, not usually."

Rachel rolled her eyes. "Gee, I wonder why."

"I have no idea," he said. "I thought women appreciated honesty. For instance, I've never thought of you as height challenged, in fact, I've always admired your long legs," he drawled, his voice slightly husky. He shifted closer, his leg resting alongside hers to measure the length of his jeans-covered thigh, knee and calf against hers. "Not so long compared to mine, though."

"Hmm, you're right." Rachel felt his body heat brand her from shoulder to calf, his jeans soft against the bare skin of her leg between her skirt and boot top.

He reached for her hand, cradling it in his palm while he carefully fitted his other hand against hers. "And your hands are downright tiny next to mine." He threaded their fingers together and lifted them to brush a kiss across her knuckles before placing her hand palm down on his thigh, his hand covering her hand to hold it there.

He leaned closer and beneath her hand, the

powerful muscles flexed and tightened. Heat raced through Rachel's veins, her body melting, swaying toward his as he slipped his free arm around her shoulders and took her mouth.

Rachel didn't protest when he lifted her and sat her on his lap facing him, her legs straddling his. He slid his hands down her back and cupped her bottom, urging her closer until they were pressed together, fused by the heat. One hand found her bare calf above her boot top, stroked up over her knee and thigh and beneath the hem of her skirt. The cotton gathered at his wrist, his fingers and warm palm moving higher until they slipped under the narrow band of silk where the waist of her bikini panties crossed her hip. His thumb stroked across her abdomen to test the sensitive indentation of her belly button and settled there.

When at last he lifted his head, she was breathless, her body burning with need. "You know we're playing with fire," he murmured, brushing his thumb over the soft skin of her belly.

"Yes," she whispered. "I know." Heat blossomed beneath her skin with each stroke of his thumb.

"You said we're adults and we can choose where we take this."

"Yes."

"Then take me to bed." His deep voice was gravelly, his eyes fierce with desire.

He was letting her choose. Despite the arousal that tightened his muscles and burned in the skin she touched, he wasn't trying to force her. Straddling his lap as she was, Rachel had no doubt that he wanted her every bit as desperately as she wanted him. Somehow that knowledge, and the fact that he was still letting her set the pace, convinced her as no amount of seduction could have.

"Come with me." She slipped off his lap and took his hand. They left the barn, the silent carnival and noisy dance hall behind, and walked across the lot to his truck.

The sliver of moon in the night sky gave just enough light to see the ruts in the alleys between vehicles. Luke pulled open the door to his pickup and lifted her inside. She automatically shifted across the bench seat to the center seat belt and buckled in.

Luke closed the door and rounded the front of the truck to slide beneath the wheel. He switched on the ignition and the powerful engine turned over, rumbling as he shifted into gear and drove slowly over the uneven ground toward the exit.

"Will it bother you if Chase finds out we spent the night together?"

"No."

"Are you sure?"

"I'm sure. Chase isn't blind, and after today, he

knows we're more than friends." Luke took her hand and threaded his fingers through hers. "I told you not to worry about this. If Chase can accept our being together without going ballistic, so can everyone else. Trust me." He pressed a kiss into her palm before placing her hand on his thigh and covering it with his.

Rachel did trust Luke. But their time together was running out. They only had tonight and the following weekend at Denver before they were through; in the real world of Wolf Creek, Kerrigans and McClouds were bitter enemies.

She knew she had to tell Luke the truth. She and her mother had duped him by offering to trade the 2500 acres for training Ransom. His expertise was worth thousands of dollars while they could never have sold the land to him or his family for more than a dollar. Her conscience wouldn't allow her to continue the deception. She'd tell him the truth in Denver.

But until then, was it so wrong to have tonight? Just one night to remember for the rest of her days? She glanced sideways. The soft glow of dashlights illuminated his features, and her fingers tightened. His gaze left the road to meet hers and his fingers pressed hers harder against his thigh.

Rachel shifted sideways and tugged on his shirt,

popping several of the pearl snaps open, and slipped her hand inside to stroke bare skin. He tensed, washboard abs flexing under her fingers as she traced the circle of his belly button.

She leaned forward and pressed her lips to his skin, warm and silky under her mouth.

"I'll give you thirty minutes to stop that." His voice rasped, thick with the same sexual hunger that coursed through her.

She tilted her head back and looked up at him. "Will it take that long to get to the motel?"

"No." He turned the wheel and left the highway.

Rachel looked up. The pink and green of the motel's neon sign winked as they drove past it.

"We're here?"

Luke didn't answer. He pulled into a parking space, switched off the engine and slid out of the truck. He leaned into the cab to grab Rachel's hand, tugging her from the seat.

He didn't speak until he'd used her key to unlock the door and then closed it behind them. The lamp Rachel had left on earlier glowed softly, the dim light making the small space intimate. Luke dropped the keys on the table and reached for her.

He caught her waist and tugged her close until her body rested against his from their hips down, the powerful muscles of his thighs supporting her. "You get one last chance," he murmured. "If you don't want this, say so now."

The lamplight cast a shadow over half his face, gently illuminating the other half. His eyes were heavy lidded, the curve of his mouth sensual and slightly swollen from the kisses they'd shared. She'd always thought he was the sexiest man she'd ever known but somehow, in the last few weeks, he'd become infinitely dear.

I'm in love with him. Stunned, Rachel could only stare at him. "Is it such a hard question?"

"No," she said hastily. "Not at all. I just…"

"Then say yes," he prompted when her voice trailed off.

Her gaze dropped to his mouth. Drawn by an undeniable force, she slipped her hands up his arms and across his shoulders to curve around his neck as she went up on tiptoe. "Yes," she breathed, just before her lips met his.

Luke groaned and crushed her mouth under his as he swung her into his arms. He reached the bed in a few strides and lowered her onto it, covering her body with his. Seconds later, he tore his mouth from hers and sat back on his heels, straddling her hips. He caught the hem of her knit top in both hands and tugged it upward. Rachel lifted and he pulled it over her head, tousling her hair, and slipped her arms free. He went suddenly still, staring down at her with hot eyes before he brushed the fingertips of his hand across the cream lace and satin of her bra.

His fingers curled around her breast and he swore under his breath before he slipped his hands under her arms and picked her up, sitting her atop the silky bedspread. He bent his head, unsuccessfully searching for the skirt zipper.

"How does this come off," he growled, frustrated when he didn't immediately find the opening.

"On the side. Here." Rachel unbuttoned and unzipped, and Luke instantly stripped the skirt down over her hips and off her feet to toss it over his shoulder. Rachel leaned forward, tugging at the hem of his T-shirt.

"Wait, honey." He shrugged out of his unbuttoned shirt and crossed his arms to grab the T-shirt hem and yank it over his head.

Rachel murmured with delight and wrapped her arms around his body, opening her mouth over the hollow of his throat where his pulse pounded, luxuriating in the silky slide of her bare skin against his.

Luke groaned and crushed her closer before he unhooked her bra and leaned back far enough to slide the straps down her arms. It followed her skirt and top, disappearing off the side of the bed, and was almost instantly joined by matching cream lace panties. Then he closed his fist in the thick mass of her hair, tugged her head back and took her mouth with his as they tumbled backward onto the mattress.

He palmed her breast and she moaned, straining against his hand. Heat streaked straight from her nipple to the cove of her thighs and her hips bucked against his, demanding, pleading.

Luke tore himself out of her arms and sat on the edge of the bed to pull off his boots. He yanked a small square packet out of his pocket and held it in his teeth while he unzipped his jeans, shoved them down his legs and kicked them off in record time.

He ripped the packet open, donned protection and lowered himself into her open arms. She curled around him, her face buried against his throat.

"Now," he groaned, wedging his thigh between hers.

Rachel barely heard him. Her whole being was focused on the joining of their bodies as he nudged against her, demanding entrance. She gasped, struggling to adjust and accept him as he pressed inexorably forward. Then he slid home and was seated deep inside her. "Are you okay?" His voice rasped in her ear, strained and nearly unrecognizable as he held himself still above her, shuddering with the effort as he waited for her answer.

"Yes," she said, pulling his mouth to hers.

Those were the last coherent words either said for long moments.

Rachel screamed when he pushed her over the edge, hardly aware that he instantly followed her.

Stunned, Luke dropped his head to the pillow and the soft silk of Rachel's hair. Muscles quivering, he barely had the presence of mind not to collapse completely on top of her.

He'd had good sex before. Whatever they'd shared was even more than great sex.

He sucked in a deep breath and she wriggled. Belatedly, he realized his weight was probably too much for her smaller frame.

"Sorry," he murmured, lifting his head, muscles flexing to shift away from her. "I'm too heavy."

"No, don't go." Her arms tightened around his neck, her thighs and calves locking around his waist to keep their hips together. "Stay."

The sensual movement banished any thought of leaving her. Luke groaned and nudged his hips against hers. Her eyes widened before her lashes lowered, the soft swollen outline of her lips curving slightly.

Luke bent and took her mouth.

This time she fell asleep almost immediately, curled against his side with his arms around her, one slim thigh over his hip, her knee nudging him.

Luke lay awake, trying to come to terms with what had just happened. Instead of erasing desire, making love to Rachel had created a desperate need to claim and keep, something he'd never felt with any other woman. Even after having her twice, he still felt an overwhelming urge to be inside her.

He glanced at the fluorescent dial on the bedside clock.

She'd only been asleep an hour. Much as he wanted to, he couldn't wake her yet. She stirred, murmuring in her sleep while she nestled closer and his arms tightened possessively.

Luke slept, but woke before dawn. The strength of his need to protect Rachel was as surprising as the rest of the night had been.

Chapter Eleven

The Denver Hills Racetrack was light years removed from the simple dirt tracks Ransom had started on weeks before. The grounds were beautifully landscaped and the clubhouse's dining areas were elegant, the theater-style seats in the indoor grandstand providing comfortable alternatives to the track-side bleachers and bench seating. Access to the barns on the track's back side was more tightly controlled than entry to the barns at the fairgrounds, and an air of tense anticipation filled the air. Instead of jeans and T-shirts, the jockeys wore silks, the brilliant blues, reds, oranges, greens and yellows creating splashes of color against the green grass and brown dirt of the paddock. David wore the Kerrigan silks, a bright blue-and-gold shirt with white pants and blue hard hat.

"Are you sure this is safe?" Rachel studied the faces of the other jockeys. Some of them looked like weathered veterans, while others appeared to be in their early twenties or late teens. But none of them looked quite as young as David.

Luke glanced down at her, following her gaze as she scanned the riders circling the paddock. "You mean for David?"

She nodded. "Everyone else looks a lot older."

"Don't worry about David," Luke reassured her. "He's young but he's seasoned. He knows what to expect and he's tough. He'll be fine."

Ransom circled the paddock with the other three-year-olds, sidling and dancing. Used to the stallion's ways, David murmured and tightened the reins, calming him.

Luke glanced at his watch. "We'd better find our seats."

They waved at David, Luke giving him a thumbs-up gesture that earned a confident grin in return, and the two left the paddock's spectator area.

They joined Chase in the bleacher seats just above the track. Rachel clenched her program in a vain effort to relieve the tension that gripped her. All around them, the crowd shifted in the bright sunlight, leaning forward to talk with friends, laughing as they consulted their race schedules or groaning as they tore up losing tickets and tossed the confetti into the air.

She jumped when the loudspeaker blared, announcing the featured race of the day. The Denver Hills Sweepstakes was the track's attempt to compete with Ruidoso Downs's famous All American Futurity race, and the half-million-dollar winner's purse was the biggest of the season. The crowd's interest heightened, focusing as all eyes turned to the row of horses and jockeys being paraded before the grandstand.

"This is it," Luke murmured in her ear.

Rachel nodded, all her attention trained on Ransom as he passed below them. His glossy hide shone in the sun, his ears swiveling as the noise swelled. David bent over his neck, and Rachel saw his lips moving as he talked to the horse.

Warm-up finished, the horses approached the starting gate. Rachel said a quick prayer, barely noticing when Luke closed his hand over hers, although she instantly gripped his fingers, aware on some level that he returned the pressure.

All went well until Ransom balked at the post.

"Oh, no," Rachel whispered, her heart in her throat.

If he refused to enter the gate, he could be disqualified.

Barely breathing, she watched as the three men working the gate joined forces, then she sighed with relief when they muscled him into his section and closed the gate on his rump.

Ransom fought David, rearing in the narrow confined space and for one heartstopping moment, Rachel thought he was going to refuse to behave. Then he dropped back on his feet and a second later, the bell sounded and the gates sprung open.

The quarter horses burst out in a pack, quickly spreading out as the leaders pulled ahead. Ransom was on the outside, with only four horses ahead of him.

"Take him inside, David," Luke murmured.

Rachel held her breath as the leaders bunched on the far turn. Ransom moved to the rail and gained ground, passing three of his competitors. When they reached the final straightaway, his speed carried him closer to the leader with each stride. He crossed the finish line a good length ahead of the other horse, winning easily, and the crowd went wild.

Luke grabbed Rachel and swung her around, kissing her soundly before letting out a whoop of victory.

"We won!" Rachel said the words aloud, dazed.

"Yup, you sure did." Chase clapped Luke on the

shoulder and grinned. "Congratulations. We'd better get down to the winner's circle and make sure Ransom doesn't take a chunk out of one of the officials."

"Good idea." Luke slipped his arm around Rachel's waist and hurried her down the steps.

David grinned, his eyes sparkling, as he sat atop Ransom. The black wasn't comfortable with the officials, who were strangers to him, and he shifted restlessly, snorting, until Luke caught his bridle and held him still. Calmer, he behaved while pictures were taken and Rachel accepted the winner's check.

"Ms. Kerrigan, what's next for your horse? Will you be taking him south to Ruidoso Downs?" An eager television reporter held a microphone toward Rachel, a cameraman filming over his shoulder.

"No," Rachel smiled into the camera. "I'm taking him home to my family's ranch in Wolf Creek, Montana, where he'll stand at stud."

"Well, that's interesting." The reporter's expression was curious. "You're not tempted to continue racing him?"

"Not at the moment. Perhaps later."

The crowd chose that moment to surge forward, and Ransom reared, snorting and huffing his displeasure. The reporter and cameraman beat a hasty retreat, putting distance between themselves and the nervous horse.

"That's it," Luke declared, softening his words with an apologetic smile. "Sorry, folks, he's not feeling sociable." He glanced at David, who nodded and immediately slipped to the ground. "We'll take him to the test barn," he told Rachel. "You can come along or meet us back at his stall."

"How long will you be?" she asked.

"Just long enough for the vet to take urine and a blood sample," he answered. "It shouldn't be more than a few minutes. They only need enough to verify he's clean of performance drugs."

"I'll go cash in my ticket and meet you at the barn."

Luke lifted an eyebrow. "You bet on Ransom?"

"Of course. And he was a long shot so my ten dollars is going to pay off big."

Luke laughed, the deep tones rich with amusement. "Then I guess you're buying the champagne tonight."

"Sure." She waggled her fingers in goodbye, watching the three men walk away with Ransom before turning to push her way through the crowd to the clubhouse.

It wasn't until she'd pocketed her winnings and was walking back to the barns that reality intruded, leaching away her euphoria.

I have to tell Luke tonight. The realization slowed her steps. She could no longer justify keeping the truth from him. And when she told him, it would be the end of everything.

She'd thought about the issue for weeks, going over and over it in an effort to find a way to tell him about the details of her grandfather's will that would make him understand and forgive her deception. Unfortunately, she couldn't find the words that might convince him.

Because there are none, the cynical side of her brain said bluntly.

She hadn't really lied to him, she just hadn't told him the whole truth.

Yeah, right, like he's going to believe that. The soft, derisive inner voice wouldn't be denied.

Rachel couldn't explain to Luke why he should forgive her, because the real truth was, she couldn't forgive herself. She loved him and she'd tricked him. How could he ever accept that? And how was she going to live the rest of her life without him?

Rachel smiled, chatted and celebrated with Luke, Chase and David through dinner and drinks at the restaurant, but she was painfully aware of the ticking of the clock as time slipped away. When they finally said goodnight, and Luke closed their hotel room door, it was all she could do to keep from running or bursting into tears.

But she wouldn't run. She owed it to Luke to tell him face-to-face; it was the least she could do. And she'd wait until he was gone before she cried.

She dropped her purse on the bedspread while Luke popped the cork on the bottle of champagne he'd brought from the bar and filled two flutes. She crossed the room and took the drink from him.

"Here's to dreams coming true." He lifted his glass and touched hers.

She sipped her champagne and set the flute carefully down on the tabletop. "Luke…"

"Mmm-hmm," he murmured, head bent as he shifted her purse from the bed to the nightstand.

"I need to talk to you."

He looked up and met her gaze. Concern edged away his smile and he cocked his head, studying her. "What's wrong?"

"Please," she gestured at the bed. "Sit down. I have something to tell you."

He dropped onto the edge of the mattress and faced her, boots planted on the floor, knees apart, elbows propped on knees, one hand cupping his untouched glass of champagne. "Okay, I'm sitting. Now tell me—what's bothering you?"

"You know my family's financial situation." She

paused and he nodded. "And you know I was desperate when I tracked you down in the bar in Billings. You were my last hope. If you'd refused to train Ransom, my mother would have lost her income from the ranch and it would have been auctioned to pay the taxes," she said. "But there were some things I didn't tell you."

Rachel forced herself to look him in the eye while she explained about her grandfather's will. Because she watched him closely, she knew the instant he understood what she was saying. His blue eyes lost their warmth, his mouth thinned, and his jaw tensed. When she stopped speaking, he stared at her for a long moment without speaking, his eyes narrowed over her as he set his champagne on the nightstand and stood.

"You scammed me." Emotionless, his voice was flat.

"I didn't tell you the whole truth when I asked you to train Ransom because I felt I had no choice." Even on her feet, facing him, Rachel felt he loomed over her. "If you'd known the truth, why would you have agreed to help me?"

"That might have been accurate in the beginning," he conceded. "But why didn't you tell me weeks ago? You had to know I was committed to seeing Ransom win."

"Because I knew you'd be angry and I didn't want to make our time together difficult."

"Difficult?" He raised an eyebrow in disbelief, his eyes icy. "Don't you mean you didn't want to risk my canceling the contract before Ransom had his shot at the sweepstakes?"

Rachel felt heat move up her throat and flush her cheeks. "That, too, I suppose."

"No wonder you always insisted we'd have to stop seeing each other once we go back to Wolf Creek," he ground out. "You only needed me until Ransom won. You're quite an actress. I actually believed you meant all the things you said in bed."

"I did." Hot tears burned but Rachel refused to let them fall. "I loved making love with you, Luke. I love you."

"Sure you do," he snarled. "It was sex, babe, just sex. You used me—I used you. Let's not confuse this with a lot of pretty words."

Pain sliced through her heart, splintering her last small hope. "I'm sorry, Luke. I never wanted to lie to you. I didn't feel I had a choice."

"People always have a choice." He stepped past her, his arm brushing hers, and hauled open the door. "For the record, Rachel, you didn't have to pay me with sex. I would have settled for the land."

And he was gone, the door slamming behind him.

Rachel caught her breath on a sob, trying to stem the tide of tears, but with the next breath, pain blindsided her and she collapsed onto the bed. She'd known he would hate her. She hadn't known how badly it would hurt.

Rachel turned off the highway onto the gravel lane leading to her ranch. The sun shone, the skies were blue, but the colors seemed muted, as if all the brightness had bled from the world.

A strange truck sat outside the house, so new it still had a sticker in the back window instead of a license plate number. She pulled up behind the silver-gray four-wheel-drive pickup, but left the engine running, planning to run into the house to let her mother know she was home before driving on to the corral to unload Ransom.

She was halfway up the sidewalk when the screen door opened and a man stepped out onto the porch. Stunned, Rachel halted abruptly.

"Hey, Rach, what took you so long to get home?" The familiar warm affection in his deep male drawl brought tears to her eyes.

"Zach!" Rachel raced up the steps. Her brother caught her, wrapping his arms around her in a hard hug. He was big and solid and warm—blessedly real and alive—and she was so relieved to see him she never wanted to let him go. "I'm so glad you're home. When did you get here? Where have you been? Why didn't you answer Mom's letters?"

"Hey, one question at a time." Zach set her on her feet and smiled down at her.

"Are you okay?" She scanned him quickly, looking for new wounds or signs of damage. He wore gray suit slacks with a black leather belt threaded through the loops, polished black boots and a pale blue dress shirt with the top three buttons undone and the cuffs folded back to his forearms. "We couldn't get any information from your boss and were so worried you were in a hospital somewhere."

"I'm fine." He held out his arms, inviting inspection. "No broken bones."

Rachel frowned at him. "Yes, but when I hugged you just now, I thought…" She ran her fingers over his shirt, just above his waistline on the left side, and traced the square outline of an extra thickness of material. "A bandage?"

"Just a small one," he admitted.

"What happened?" she demanded.

"I zigged when I should have zagged, and the other guy had a knife."

Rachel felt the blood drain out of her face, anxiety welling. "But you said you were all right."

"I am." Zach shrugged. "The doc stitched me closed and sent me back to work. Like I said, no big deal."

Rachel searched his face. She knew he kept much of what happened on the job from her and their mother and she probably would never convince him to tell her what really happened. But he was tanned, seemingly healthy and on the mend, despite the knife wound. She'd have to be satisfied with that. "I'm not sure I believe you, but since I can't see blood and broken bones anywhere, I'll let you get away with it. This time. But you still haven't told me where you've been for the last few months."

"Let's go inside. Mom's making coffee and I might as well answer your questions at the same time as hers."

"I have to unload Ransom first."

"I'll help."

Rachel looked at the sheen on his black boots and shook her head. "You'll get dirty."

He laughed and ruffled her hair. "I might as well get used to it, don't you think?"

They slipped into a familiar rhythm, working together to unload Ransom and turn him out into the pasture behind the barn. The quarter horse kicked up his heels and raced across the open ground, clearly delighted to be out of the confines of the trailer.

They watched him for a few minutes before walking back to the house.

Zach pulled open the screen door and waved her in ahead of him.

"When did you get home?" She stepped inside, and they walked down the hall to the kitchen together.

"About an hour ago."

"I assume that's your truck parked outside?"

Zach nodded. "I flew into Billings, caught a taxi to the nearest truck dealership and bought it. I wanted my own vehicle and thought it would be easier to get it on the way home."

"Nice wheels. Does this mean you're staying?"

"Yes. I quit my job and for better or worse, I'm home for good."

Rachel felt a surge of relief and elation. For the first time, she realized she'd harbored a slight concern that Zach would choose to remain in his dangerous, exciting career rather than return to take up the quieter life of a rancher.

"There you two are," Judith said as they entered the kitchen.

"Hi, Mom." Rachel gave her mother a swift hug. The tension she'd felt in her mother for the past few months was gone, erased by Zach's return.

"Have you told her?" Judith asked Zach.

Rachel stepped back, glancing from her mother to her brother. "Told me what?"

"Let's sit down and get comfortable," Judith said. "We have a lot to talk about."

Slipping into a chair, Rachel waited impatiently while Judith sat and Zach joined them. He took a mug of coffee from his mother and sipped before answering Rachel.

"I wish I'd hadn't been out of contact," he began. "It's a damn shame you and Mom have been so worried about money, because I can cover the debts."

Rachel stared at him, speechless. "You can? But how…?"

"I invested the money Grandmother left me plus I've been saving every dime I could since I turned eighteen. My long-term plan was always to come home to Montana and buy a ranch somewhere." He glanced around the kitchen, a mix of emotions roiling in his eyes. "I never thought I'd be lucky enough to inherit part of Kerrigan Holdings. But since Granddad left it to me, the money I've saved and invested can be spent here. If the amount Mom estimated is correct, I have enough to pay the taxes and operate the properties for us until we're back on our feet."

Shock held Rachel frozen for a moment before she burst into tears. She caught a glimpse of Zach's appalled face before she dropped her head into her hands and tried to swallow her sobs.

"What's wrong?"

Judith took Rachel's hands in hers and gently tugged them away from her face, tucking a tissue into one palm. "Dry your eyes, Rachel. I had the same reaction." She looked at Zach. "I'm sure it's just the sudden relief from the stress of worrying about how we were going to manage. The past few months have been hard on us both. Your news, coming on the heels of the $500,000 Ransom won last night, is almost too much to take in."

"Five hundred thousand dollars?" Zach's eyes widened. "You told me he won in Denver, but I didn't realize the purse was that big."

"He won the sweepstakes." Judith beamed with delight, and caught Rachel in a tight hug.

I didn't need to lie to Luke—tricking him into helping me wasn't necessary. Rachel struggled to rein in her emotions. She wiped her eyes and managed a wobbly smile. "Mom's right, Zach, these are tears of relief."

"Okay." He scrubbed a hand down his face and sighed. "Damn, I'm so sorry you two have had such a bad time."

"None of that matters, now that you're home." Judith patted his hand and smiled. "Now," she said briskly, sitting up a bit straighter. "We have to decide what to do about the land we promised to Luke."

"What do you mean?" Rachel's gaze flicked from her mother's face to Zach's and back again.

"I explained to Zach the terms of the contract we signed with Luke in return for his training Ransom."

"From what you told me about Granddad's will, it sounds like you can sign off on the deed, Mom." Zach waited for Judith's nod of confirmation. "Much as I hate to lose land, it also appears Granddad was making a statement."

Rachel and Judith exchanged glances. "We think so," Rachel said.

Zach's eyes narrowed. "If I understand what you told me correctly, Granddad's will stipulated the disputed acres can only be sold to the McClouds." His gaze was incisive when he met Rachel's. "I'm guessing Granddad either knew or suspected Lonnie was involved in the Harper kid's death."

Rachel nodded, glancing at her mother. "That's the same conclusion we reached."

Zach swore under his breath and shoved away from the table, pacing to the window to stare out. The silence stretched for a long moment, then he turned, his features grimly resolute. "It seems to me we're honor-bound to deed the land to Luke McCloud. We signed a contract and he fulfilled his part of the agreement. There's no question Ransom's stud fees will go a long way toward making it easier to get our shares of Granddad's property back on their feet."

Rachel realized she'd been holding her breath and she released it in a sigh of relief. "I agree."

Judith nodded. "So do I. I had the documents drawn up a few weeks ago, in case we needed them. Arnie Cline has them in his office file."

"I need to talk to Arnie about the legal aspects of my share of the property so I'll drive into town tomorrow. You can meet me at his office and sign the papers, Mom. I'll buy you lunch afterward."

"I'll go with you," Rachel said. "I want to tuck a note to Luke into the envelope with the deed."

Rachel spent an hour that evening composing a letter to Luke. She finally settled on a few brief sentences explaining that she was enclosing a personal check for the first payment on the debt she felt she owed him for his normal charges to train and race a quarter horse. She didn't know exactly what the total bill might be, so she made a rough estimate and asked him to advise her if her guess was wrong.

The next morning she accompanied Zach to the lawyer's office and while he was discussing the legal entanglements surrounding their grandfather's will, Rachel went to the post office and mailed the envelope with her note, check and the land deed to Luke.

Chapter Twelve

Three days later Luke pulled up next to the big metal mailbox on the highway and shifted into Neutral with the engine idling while he scooped the stack of letters and periodicals from the box. Then he drove down the lane to the ranch house, parked and went inside. He dropped the stack of mail on the table in the kitchen and crossed to the refrigerator to get a cold beer.

The screen door on the utility porch slapped shut and Chase walked into the room.

Luke was in a foul mood. He had been ever since Rachel confessed she'd lied to convince him to train Ransom. Anger seethed under the surface, and his temper strained against a short leash. He'd slammed out of the hotel, driven straight through the night to reach home and then worked long hours at the dirtiest, sweatiest jobs on the ranch in an effort to rid himself of the rage that churned in his gut.

But instead his behavior had fanned the anger, nursed it, and he liked it that way, because if it burned off, all he'd have left would be the pain of betrayal and loss.

"Anything interesting in the mail?"

"I don't know, haven't looked at it." Luke grabbed a bottle off the shelf, slammed the fridge door and twisted off the top.

Chase stood at the table, thumbing through the envelopes and dropping the magazines in a pile to one side. "Well," he said slowly, "this is interesting."

"What?" Luke tossed the bottle cap into the trash can and lifted the beer to his lips.

"A letter from Rachel Kerrigan addressed to you."

Luke lowered the bottle without drinking, his eyes narrowing at Chase. His brother held a letter-size manila envelope in his hands, his expression neutral as he turned it over, glanced at the back, then held it out. Luke set his beer down on the table and took the envelope from Chase, glancing at the return address before he ripped it open. Inside, a single sheet of stationery was folded around a legal-size document. When Luke removed them, a check slipped free and fluttered to the tabletop.

"What the hell?" Luke picked up the check and scanned it swiftly. The personal check on Rachel's account was payable to him in the sum of two hundred dollars. Baffled, he unfolded the other papers. The legal sheet was a document deeding the twenty-five hundred acres of land to him and was signed by Judith Kerrigan.

He dropped it on the table and unfolded the letter. The first line had his eyes widening in shock. By the third line he was swearing. "She signed it 'Best regards.'" He crumpled the letter in his fist. "Best regards."

"I take it the letter is from Rachel?" Chase asked.

"Yeah." Luke cursed and paced across the kitchen.

"She's not what I expected," Chase commented. "And you're happier when she's around."

Luke halted and stared at his brother.

"Maybe you two should ignore the feud and forget what our families think—decide for yourself what's between you and where you want to go from here."

"You don't know the whole story," Luke muttered.

Chase shrugged. "I've seen the two of you

together. I'm guessing whatever she did is worth fighting about and then getting past." He picked up the legal paper from the kitchen table and scanned it, then looked up at Luke. "And they followed through. They paid you with the deed to the homestead acres."

"Yeah."

"So, what are you going to do about the note from Rachel?" Chase leaned against the counter, arms across his chest, a half smile on his face.

Luke glared at him. Chase's question cut through the anger, and suddenly Luke knew exactly what he was going to do—what he'd wanted to do ever since he'd stormed out of the hotel room in Denver.

He crammed the note in his pocket and grabbed his hat off the peg next to the door.

"Hey, where are you going?" Chase called after him.

"To get Rachel," Luke answered. "She's going to marry me if I have to tie her up and keep her that way until she says yes."

"It's about time." Chase's laughter sounded over the slap of the screen door slamming shut as Luke jogged down the steps and headed for his truck, parked just outside the fence.

He ignored all speed limits, and within fifteen minutes he strode up the porch steps and knocked on

Rachel's door. When he didn't get an immediate response, he knocked again.

Light footsteps sounded inside the house, and Rachel's mother pushed open the door. "Luke?" The astonishment in her voice reflected the surprise written on her face.

"Afternoon, Mrs. Kerrigan," Luke removed his hat and nodded politely. "Is Rachel home?"

"Why, yes, she is. I'll get her—would you like to come in?"

"No, thank you. I'll wait here." Bad enough he was standing on the enemy's porch, Luke thought.

"Very well." Judith smiled uncertainly and closed the screen door.

Luke waited impatiently, half turning to look across the ranch yard. A man exited the barn and walked toward the silver pickup parked at the corrals. Luke hadn't seen Zach Kerrigan in years, not since they'd gone to high school together, but he recognized him instantly.

Behind him the screen door squeaked. He turned back just as Rachel stepped onto the porch. She was wearing white shorts and a yellow tank top, her bare arms and legs tanned, leather sandals on her slim feet. Her hair was caught up in a ponytail high on her head.

She shifted, a faint blush staining the smooth skin

over her cheekbones, and Luke realized he'd been silently staring. He cleared his throat, buoyed by a fresh wave of resolve.

"I need to talk to you."

"You do?" She eyed him warily, arms crossed protectively over her chest. "If this is about the check…"

"No," he said abruptly. "At least, not directly."

"Then what—"

"It's a business proposition."

"I don't know, Luke…"

Frustrated, Luke was tempted to pick her up and carry her off but he restrained himself. "We can't talk here. Come back to the ranch with me. It's quiet there."

"I'm not sure that's a good idea." She looked torn.

"All I want is a few minutes of your time." Luke easily read the indecision in her expressive features. "I listened to you in Billings, Rachel. You owe me the same consideration."

Her gaze was troubled and she bit her lip. "All right," she said reluctantly. "I'll be right back. I want to let Mom know where I'm going."

Elation surged through Luke. At least she'd agreed to listen to him.

She rejoined him on the porch. Luke stalked beside her down the sidewalk, steeling himself when he glanced across the ranch yard and saw Zach walking toward them. "Your brother's home."

Rachel's gaze followed his, and a small, spontaneous smile curved her mouth. "Yes, thank goodness." With a quick flash of worry she glanced from Zach to Luke. "You won't…"

"Don't worry," Luke reassured her, briefly resting his hand on her forearm. "Nothing's going to happen. I didn't come here to fight with your brother."

Zach stopped several feet away, his eyes raking Rachel before he looked at Luke. "Luke."

"Zach." Luke's voice was as neutral as Zach's.

"What's going on?" Zach addressed his question to Rachel.

"I'm going with Luke." To Luke's surprise, Rachel's voice was firm and she didn't give her brother an explanation, nor did her eyes waver from his. "I won't be long."

Zach looked at her for a moment, then switched his gaze to Luke. Luke didn't comment, merely returning the level stare.

Then Zach nodded, his face enigmatic as he looked at his sister. "Be careful." He touched the brim of his hat and walked past them to the house.

Rachel's sigh of relief reached Luke's ears, and he smiled. For whatever reason, her brother had decided to remain uninvolved. Come to think of it, he realized, her mother hadn't been hostile, either.

He pulled open the passenger door of his truck, caught Rachel by the waist and lifted her in. Her quick, indrawn breath told him she wasn't immune to his touch, and he felt a fierce gladness that she felt the same electricity that struck him.

Then he slammed the door, rounded the hood of the truck and slid behind the wheel.

"I don't want to talk and drive at the same time," he twisted the key in the ignition, and the engine turned over with a rumble. "It's only fifteen minutes to my place."

Rachel murmured her assent and Luke shifted into gear, leaving the Section Ten ranch buildings behind.

Tension gripped Rachel. She stole a sideways glance at Luke, his profile all hard angles with no softness. She dreaded the argument that was sure to come when they reached his house but felt she owed it to him to listen. By the time Luke parked outside the house and ushered her up the sidewalk and through the door, her nerves were stretched tight.

He gestured toward the sofa. "Have a seat."

"No, thanks. I'd rather stand." Arms folded, she braced herself for what she knew would be a blistering indictment.

Instead Luke thrust his hands into the front pockets of his jeans and stared at her.

She couldn't stand it when he didn't immediately

speak. "Look, I'm sure you're going to yell at me about the check I sent you, so just get it over with."

Luke looked startled but then his eyes narrowed, temper darkening the blue to navy. "All right, let's talk about the check. You paid me with the deed to the land. Where did you get the harebrained idea that you owed me more?"

"We both know I couldn't have traded the land to you for more than one dollar. Those are the terms set by Granddad's will. I owe you the market value of your time for training Ransom, and that far exceeds a buck."

"We had an agreement—the land for training Ransom. Neither of us said anything about market value for my services."

"I don't care," Rachel said stubbornly. "I'm going to pay the going rate for your services with a check every month from now until the debt is paid off."

A smile quirked Luke's mouth. "Honey, at the rate you're going, you'll still owe me money a hundred years from now."

"I don't care. This is important to me."

"I can see that." He stepped closer, his fingers gentle when they tucked an errant strand of hair behind her ear and returned to stroke down her cheek. "I have a better idea for clearing the debt you seem to believe you owe me."

"Oh?" Rachel was having trouble thinking with his fingertips smoothing over her skin and the warmth of his body only inches from hers.

"Marry me."

Shock rippled through her, leaving her stunned and speechless. His eyes were dark with emotion and a hint of uncertainty. *He's serious*, she realized. *He actually wants me to marry him.*

And she burst into tears.

Luke's panicked expression was barely visible through her blurred vision, but fortunately, he instantly wrapped his arms around her and pulled her close.

"Hey, I'm sorry. Don't cry." He smoothed his palm over the crown of her head, fingers tangling in her ponytail, and pressed a kiss against her temple. "Damn, honey, don't cry. We don't have to get married if you don't want to. We can live together first, if you want."

Rachel, her face tight against the warmth of his throat, smiled at the reluctant concession in his deep voice.

"You want to live together?" She asked, her voice muffled.

"Hell, no." His instant denial was reassuring. "But I'll take what I can get."

She pushed against his chest, and his arms loosened slightly, just enough to let her lean back and look up at him. He was frowning, his eyes fierce. "Won't your family object?"

"Maybe. But once they know Chase approves, they'll come around. What about your family? I know Harlan and Lonnie won't ever accept me."

Rachel's mouth drooped, then firmed. "No, I think that's too much to hope for. But my mother won't object, and after seeing Zach's response today, I think he might get used to the idea, eventually."

"I'm not saying it'll be easy, but we'll work it out. And who knows, maybe our kids will make their grandparents let go of old grudges."

"Do you really think so?"

"I know so." Luke's voice lowered, rough with emotion. "Say yes, honey. I've loved you since we were kids, and we've waited long enough. Marry me."

Fresh tears welled up in Rachel's eyes, spilling over to slide slowly down her cheeks, but this time Luke didn't panic. Instead he carefully wiped them away with the pad of his thumb, his smile tender. "Say yes, honey."

She whispered, "Yes" against his lips just before he stole her breath with a fierce kiss and swung her into his arms, striding down the hall to his bedroom.

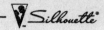

SPECIAL EDITION™

PRESENTING A NEW MINISERIES BY
RaeANNE THAYNE:

The Cowboys of Cold Creek

BEGINNING WITH
LIGHT THE STARS
April 2006

Widowed rancher Wade Dalton relied
on his mother's help to raise three small
children—until she eloped with "life coach"
Caroline Montgomery's grifter father! Feeling
guilty, Caroline put her Light the Stars
coaching business on hold to help the angry
cowboy…and soon lit a fire in his heart.

DON'T MISS THESE ADDITIONAL BOOKS IN THE SERIES:
DANCING IN THE MOONLIGHT, May 2006
DALTON'S UNDOING, June 2006

SPECIAL EDITION™

DON'T MISS THE FIRST BOOK IN

PATRICIA McLINN's

EXCITING NEW SERIES

Seasons in a Small Town

WHAT ARE FRIENDS FOR?

April 2006

When tech mogul Zeke Zeekowsky returned for his hometown's Lilac Festival, the former outsider expected a hero's welcome. Instead, his high school fling, policewoman Darcie Barrett, mistook him for a wanted man and handcuffed him! But the software king and the small-town girl were quick to make up....

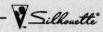

SPECIAL EDITION™

RETURN TO HART VALLEY IN

HER BABY'S HERO

BY

KAREN SANDLER

Elementary school teacher Ashley Rand
was having CEO Jason Kerrigan's baby.
Even though they came from different
worlds, each was running from trouble.
So when Jason rented the Victorian house
of Ashley's dreams, they both believed life
would slow down. Until they found out
Ashley was having twins!

Available April 2006
at your favorite retail outlet.